beautiful COLLISION

A. M. KUSI

This book is a work of fiction. Names, places, characters, organizations, events, and incidents are either products of the authors' imaginations or are used fictitiously. Any resemblance to actual persons, living or dead, or to businesses, companies, events, institutions, or locales is completely coincidental. Any trademarks, product names, service marks, and named features are assumed to be the property of their respective owners and are only used for references.

Published by A. M. Kusi 2021

amkusinovels@gmail.com

Visit our website at www.amkusi.com

Editor: Kelly Golland of CREATING ink

Sensitivity Edit: Renita McKinney of A Book A Day

Proofreader: Judy's Proofreading

Cover Design: Regina Wamba of ReginaWamba.com

ISBN: 978-1-949781-23-6

OTHER BOOKS BY A. M. KUSI

A Fallen Star (eBook FREE on all retailers)

(Book 1 in The Shattered Cove Series)

Glass Secrets

(Book 2 in The Shattered Cove Series)

Defying Gravity

(Book 3 in The Shattered Cove Series)

The Lighthouse Inn

(Book 4 in The Shattered Cove series)

His True North

(Book 5 in The Shattered Cove series)

In The Grey

(Book 6 in The Shattered Cove series)

Brave Love

(Book 7 in The Shattered Cove series)

The Orchard Inn (eBook FREE on all retailers)

(Book 1 in The Orchard Inn Romance Series)

Conflict of Interest

(Book 2 in The Orchard Inn Romance Series)

Her Perfect Storm

(Book 3 in The Orchard Inn Romance Series)

One Holiday Kiss (eBook FREE on all retailers)

(A Shattered Cove Short Story)

For a complete list of all our books, visit:

WWW.AMKUSI.COM/BOOKS

"You are not a victim for sharing your story. You are a survivor setting the world on fire with your truth. And you never know who needs your light, your warmth and raging courage."
— Alex Elle

"Maybe it's actually a good thing that your mom isn't proud of you."
— Mother Wound Project

TABLE OF CONTENTS

GET A FREE SHORT NOVEL

Join our newsletter to get a FREE story that's not available on any retailer. Plus updates about new releases, giveaways, pre-orders, sneak peeks, and more.

Visit the website below to join now.

WWW.AMKUSI.COM/NEWSLETTER

TRIGGER WARNING

This book has sensitive subject matter that deals with SA that may be triggering for some.

1

———

MADDY

Crash!

"Mommy!"

Maddy's heart raced as she jolted out of bed. The tiny room quickly came into focus. Her son's tiny hands grasped her leg. Joshua trembled.

"Maaaadyyyy," a man's voice called from behind the flimsy front door that was now hanging half off the frame. *Oh. God! No.* A voice she knew all too well.

"Come on, sweetheart. You've teased me enough."

Men always thought because she was a woman, they were somehow entitled to her body. *Fuck them. Fuck him.* Never again would she be a victim.

He grunted and the sound of wood splintering followed. He was almost through. Fear wound around her like a snake, as adrenaline flooded her veins. Weapon, she needed a weapon. All she had was the pepper spray on her keychain, conveniently located by the door. She couldn't risk it.

"Mommy!" Joshua cried again. She was his only protection in the world. What was she going to do? They were boxed

I

in this tiny grungy apartment and a monster was blocking the only way out.

Protect Josh. "Shhh, it's okay, baby." Tears sprung to her eyes as she shakily reached for her phone and dialed emergency services. She tucked her son into the tiny closet. "Stay here, baby. Close your ears. Don't come out until Mommy says to."

He screamed and clung to her. A sob tore through her throat as the operator picked up.

"Nine-one-one, what's your emergency?"

"Help me, a man has broken into my house and he's trying to attack me and my son." She rattled off her address. Would the police actually come? They hardly ever did to this side of town.

"MADDY! Fuck!" Scott yelped and then another loud crash thudded through the room.

Someone help us.

Just like her pleas when she was eighteen and trapped with the Holt cousins, this nightmare wouldn't end. No one was coming to save her. And she was the only thing standing between her son and this slimy fuck.

She pulled away from her crying son and rushed to their tiny kitchen to grab a knife. Her hands grasped the cool metal handle as two beefy arms locked around her, pinning her against the counter.

"That's no way to greet a man who worked so hard to get to you." Scott's acrid breath burst beside her. She turned her head away, sucking in oxygen as the plywood counter bit into her hips.

"I called the cops and they're on their way. You better leave. I don't think even your uncle can get you out of this."

Scott laughed. "By the time they get here, I'll have got

what I wanted. What, my cock isn't good enough for you, bitch?"

Clang!

Scott's weight fell on her before he crumpled to the floor. Maddy didn't waste time; she spun around, ready to fight.

There, in the shadows of her apartment, was the small older lady who lived next door and babysat Joshua for her. "Mrs. Feines?"

"You better go, dear, before he wakes up." She nodded behind her.

Go. Yes, she needed to get out of here. "Thank you." Maddy dashed into the other room, scooping up her shaking child who clung to her neck for dear life.

"Mama, is the bad man gone?"

"Close your eyes, sweetheart. Go to your happy safe place in your mind. Go to the cloud room, okay?"

"Otay." He laid his head against her as she used one hand to open a backpack and stuff every piece of clothing he owned in it and the few cars he played with. She hefted the bag over her shoulder and grabbed the torn duffle and filled it with the few things she owned. That was it—everything they needed in two bags. Her work things were in her car already. She just needed one last thing. Opening her freezer, she dug into the far back and pulled out the ice cream carton. She opened it and retrieved the wad of cash she kept inside.

"Let's go, sweet boy. Keep your eyes closed."

She turned to the older woman still standing guard with her cast-iron skillet over Scott's body as he moaned.

"Go on." Mrs. Feines ushered her out the door, quickly disappearing back into her apartment.

"Thank you!" Maddy called again, before racing for her car. She buckled her son in with shaky hands and slid into the driver's seat, locking the doors and cranking the ignition.

She backed out of the parking lot and headed towards the highway.

"Where are we going, Mama?" Joshua's voice was shaky and small.

Her chest squeezed. God, she hated that he'd heard all of that. Where could she go? She had nothing and no one. Her son needed more than what she'd been able to give him. When was the last time she'd truly felt safe?

A flash of Turner's face popped into her mind. His dark tan skin and light blue eyes looking at her like he actually saw her under the facade she put up for everyone else. But then a few days later, she had called him when she needed him most and he hadn't even picked up.

However, Gerry had. Turner's dad had been there when she was at her worst and brought her to safety. He was the one man in the world she could count on. That night with him was the last time she'd felt safe. She shook her head and shoved that memory aside. Maybe it was time to stop running.

"Mama?" Joshua asked.

"We're going to Shattered Cove." *Home.*

"Will there be bad men there too?"

Her heart broke a little more. She'd tried to do right by him, raising him alone after his father had happily signed away his rights—no doubt easy, since he was still married to another woman. Something that bastard had failed to mention the whole time Maddy had been busy falling in love with him.

Maddy glanced in the rearview mirror. "Go to sleep, little man. It's a long drive."

"Luff you, Mama."

Emotion swelled in her throat. "I love you too."

Joshua was the greatest gift she'd ever been given, and for the first time in her life, someone loved her. Someone chose her. And she'd do whatever she needed to do in order to protect her son. Even if that meant facing the boy she once loved, who was now a man who probably still hadn't forgiven her. If Turner found out the truth of that night, would he hate her even more?

There was only one way to find out.

2

TURNER

Turner yawned and rubbed his eyes as the cab drove him past the sign for Shattered Cove. He might have still been a little drunk from the going-away party the guys threw him. He'd barely made his plane from Florida to Boston.

He rolled down the window and let the warm breeze of his hometown blow over him. His time in the Navy was done, and just in time to take over his father's landscaping business.

A few minutes later, the cabbie pulled up in front of a small white house with blue shutters. It was too dark to see, but the flowers around the home were sure to be immaculate. *A man must always have his house in order before anything else.* His father's words echoed in his mind as he paid the cab driver a hefty sum and tried not to wince.

There was nothing left for him in Jacksonville anymore. He didn't see the point of waiting for a later flight and making his dad drive all the way to the airport.

Turner grabbed his big military duffle bag. All he owned fit into the worn fabric.

The low hum of the cab disappeared as he lifted his face to the full moon and took a deep breath. This was his chance to start fresh. He'd traveled all over the world, but he'd never quite felt he belonged anywhere but here in Shattered Cove, New Hampshire.

Pulling out a set of keys, he walked to the door and let himself in. Trying to be quiet, he toed off his boots and didn't bother turning a light on as he moved up the stairs. He had the layout of this house memorized. It hadn't changed once in the twenty-six years he'd been alive.

He skipped over the step that always creaked and smiled. As a teen, he'd learned to avoid it when sneaking out of the house.

Turner crept down the hall to his old bedroom. He sighed and set his bag down with a quiet thunk. *I'm just going to fall into bed and sleep for three days.*

Turner pulled the shirt over his head and left it in a pile on the floor. He unbuttoned his pants, letting them slip off before he adjusted himself in his boxers. Reaching out, he pulled the covers off the bed and froze. His breath caught in his lungs. Turner rubbed his eyes, making sure he wasn't seeing things.

What the fuck is a woman doing in my bed?

He leaned closer, squinting in the dim light. *No. It couldn't be.* Moonlight glowed off her fair skin. Her long dirty blonde hair fanned over her pillow.

There was no mistaking that sexy pout or the button nose.

Madeline Miller was in his bed. *What is she doing here?*

Why hadn't his dad told him she was back in town, and staying at his house no less? The last time he'd seen her . . . Maddy had been bullying Turner's best friend, Jasmine, and shredding the girl to ribbons. Old anger heated his body. His eyes roamed over her lithe figure once more. She was curled into herself, one hand under her pillow and the other under her cheek. His cock jerked. Maddy had always been beautiful, but the eight years she'd been gone had turned her into a stunner.

Stop staring at her like a pervert. But what else was he supposed to do? It was three in the morning, too early to wake his dad up and ask what the hell was going on. *Why hadn't he told me when he knew I was coming this week?* Turner grimaced. *Is she seeing my father?* His stomach churned.

Why else would Princess Maddy come down from her throne and slum it with commoners like the Walkers and their bargain store sheets rather than the Egyptian cotton she was no doubt used to?

Turner was going to get to the bottom of this. He reached out towards her shoulder, but before he made contact, she jerked up.

Something wet sprayed into his eyes before they burned with liquid fire.

"Ow! Fuck!"

Maddy gripped his shoulders. Maybe she realized her mistake and was trying to help?

Searing pain erupted in his groin before he dropped to his knees. "FUUUUUUUUUUCK!"

The bedroom door swung open and Maddy darted out of the room, screaming.

Turner hunched over in pain, fighting the urge to wipe his eyes, but that would only make it worse.

A shotgun clicked, cocked and ready for use. Turner spun around and held up his hands.

"What's going on?" His father's voice boomed.

"It's me! Jesus Christ, don't shoot! It's Turner!"

The light switched on as hot tears mingled with pepper spray and flowed down his cheeks. He coughed. It was so strong.

"Oh my God." Maddy gasped, sounding like she was somewhere out in the hall.

"Mommy? Is that a bad man?" a little voice asked also sounding farther away.

Mommy? Maddy was a mother?

"It's okay, baby," she soothed.

Turner blinked his eyes open, catching sight of the blurry three figures before he slammed them closed again.

"Sorry, you weren't supposed to be here until tomorrow," his dad pointed out.

"Surprise," Turner deadpanned.

"What the hell were you thinking, sneaking in the house like that and scaring the girl half to death?" Dad demanded.

Turner got to his feet, still cupping his throbbing balls. "I didn't expect someone to be in my bed. It's not my fault. She's the one who pepper-sprayed me and kneed me in the nuts." Turner pointed to the general vicinity he guessed she was. "Maddy might have stolen your only chance for grandkids." Turner bent over, resting his hands on his knees. "I need liquid antacid for my eyes, and ice for my balls."

His dad huffed.

"I'll get it," Maddy offered. "You go get back into bed, sweetie, and I'll be right in."

"But, Mommy—"

"It's okay. I'll take the little guy." His dad's voice softened. What the hell was going on?

"Can we wead a 'tory?" the boy asked.

"Joshua Gerald Miller," Maddy warned.

Gerald? As in, Gerry? As in, Turner's dad?

Turner's mouth dropped open, which made him suck in more of the pepper residue and start coughing. *Was this kid his little brother?* His stomach churned.

Footsteps padded down the hall. Hopefully Maddy with that antacid and ice.

"Come on, Josh. Papa Walker will read you two stories, but shhh, don't tell your mom. Turner, we'll talk in the morning."

A small giggle erupted from the little boy as the sound of his father's heavy footsteps disappeared down the hall towards the spare room.

A minute later, Maddy returned. Cold plastic touched his hand.

"Here's some ice. Can you walk to the bathroom so I can pour the antacid over your eyes?"

He grunted and got to his feet.

She coughed. "Wow, that's really strong."

"No kidding," he snapped and walked towards the general direction of the doorway.

Her small hand pressed against his lower back, sending zings of electricity shooting through him. A small gasp left her lips, but she didn't remove her palm. Was this a side effect from the pepper spray? Or was she affected by his touch too?

She guided him towards the bathroom. "Turn right. Now step in the tub."

He lifted his leg and climbed in.

"I need you to sit so I can pour it over."

He obeyed, setting the ice on his groin. "You have to mix it with water in a fifty-fifty mixture and then pour it."

"Um . . . okay." The sound of plastic hitting the edge of the tub was followed by the gurgle of liquid. She turned the bath on.

Cold water poured over his feet as he hissed and tucked his legs closer to his body on the other end of the tub.

"Sorry."

"Somehow, I doubt that," he grumbled.

As soon as the water turned warm, she got what she needed and shut it off.

"Sit forward and tip your head back," she instructed.

He scooted closer and tilted his head towards the ceiling. Warm liquid dripped over his eyes as her other hand cupped the back of his head. Her soft touch made his cock jerk. *Now is really not the time. And definitely not with her.* He blinked his eyes open, trying to help flush the pepper residue out.

She repeated the process until the burning dulled and he could see once again, though his vision was still blurry.

She sat on the ground outside the tub. Her hair fell over her shoulders as concern marred her expression. "I'm really sorry, Turner. You scared me. I thought . . . well, I didn't know it was you."

"Who would have thought I would return to my own room?" Sarcasm dripped from every syllable. He was exhausted, in pain, and confused as fuck. Not to mention angry.

Her gaze dropped to his bare chest, her cheeks blushing the color of her rosebud mouth. Her attention flickered back to his face sheepishly. "Your dad said you were living in Florida."

"As of today, I'm back. I didn't tell him I was coming early. And what a welcome home it was," he gritted out.

Her shoulders slumped. "Sorry. I guess he didn't tell you my son and I were staying here either."

His gaze narrowed on her frustratingly gorgeous face. She might seem soft and innocent, but he'd been fooled by those doe eyes before and gotten burned—badly. "Why are you here?"

Her chest rose as if she were taking a deep breath as she stared at the edge of the tub. "I needed a place to stay for a while."

"Shouldn't you go to Mommy and Daddy's and stay in their big mansion? Not sure our humble abode is up to your standards, princess."

Maddy flinched, and he hated that it tore at his heart. Anger swirled in his chest, unfurling to his limbs like a fire-breathing dragon. This woman had nearly broken his best friend in high school, and on prom night, no less. She'd fooled Turner into thinking there was a heart under that snobby picture-perfect exterior. Now she'd shown up with a kid named after his father. What the hell was he supposed to think? Or feel? What other reason would Maddy Miller have for living with his father? Had she somehow convinced him the kid was his? Or had she tricked him into thinking she would be interested in him romantically? Would his dad fall for that? No, surely not. *But Dad is lonely.* Had that made him blind to the likes of Maddy's charm?

One thing was for sure. Maddy Miller was a manipulative pretentious woman, and he was going to expose her for the charlatan she was.

3

MADDY

Maddy plated the last of the pancakes and set them on the center of the small table off to the side of the kitchen.

"Thank you, sweetheart." Gerry offered her a kind smile before he sipped his coffee.

"It's the least I could do." She picked one of the smaller pancakes and set it on her son's plate, cutting it into squares before drizzling some maple syrup over it.

"Mmmm." Josh's eyes widened as he rubbed his hands together like a little evil genius.

Maddy chuckled and leaned in to kiss his chubby cheek.

Josh stuffed the first bite of his breakfast into his mouth, but his smile dropped as tingles raced up Maddy's arms. The energy in the room shifted and she didn't have to turn around to know Turner had entered.

Josh reached out for her. Maddy slipped her hand into his and forced a smile. "Joshy, this is Turner, Papa Walker's son."

Josh flicked his gaze between his mother and the man in the doorway. "He yelled weally loud last night."

Gerry burst out laughing. "He did, didn't he? He's a baby when it comes to pain. Don't know how he survived so long in the military."

Josh giggled. "You called him a baby!"

Maddy turned towards a red and puffy-eyed Turner, who pushed off the side of the door, uncrossing his arms as he slipped into the seat between Josh and his father. Grumbling, he grabbed a cup of coffee and poured himself some. "You'd be screaming too if you got pepper-sprayed and nearly lost the family jewels."

Even grumpy and disheveled, the man was sex on a stick. His light blue eyes narrowed on her, and a flash of guilt lit her chest.

Maddy took the only seat available, across from him. Butterflies flitted through her belly. Her gaze flicked back to his coarse stubble, a heavy five o'clock shadow. It had rubbed against her arm last night in the tub, sending a shiver through her. After all this time apart, she'd been hoping he would affect her less, not more.

He sipped his coffee, his strong square jaw flexing. As he sat next to his father, it was clear the two men were almost twins. Turner was a few shades lighter than his amber-hued father, but their features were so similar. His thick, curly blond hair and blue eyes must have come from his white mother. Her picture hung on the walls in the living room, but Gerry didn't mention her too much—just said that she was no longer with them.

Breakfast didn't get any less awkward. She cleaned up after them, despite Gerry's protests, while Turner sat quietly stewing in the corner, his gaze rarely leaving her. By the time she kissed Josh goodbye before he slipped to the backyard to play catch with Gerry, her heart was racing. She pressed her hand on her chest in an attempt to slow it, but it was no use.

Maddy opened the door to the office downstairs, headed down the steps and sat behind the desk. She turned on the computer and pulled up the accounting software, trying to find where she left off.

"What the fuck do you think you're doing?"

Maddy jumped. Her eyes darted to the door where a fuming Turner stood. His hard glare leveled on her. If looks could kill, she'd be flayed alive.

"I-I'm doing some bookkeeping."

He shook his head and crossed his arms. "No way. My father wouldn't be stupid enough to give someone like you access to the business accounts."

She stood, straightening her spine and lifted her chin. "Someone like me?"

Turner stepped closer, crowding her space until all she could smell was his intoxicating spicy scent. She backed up but he followed until her back hit the bookshelf behind her. She had nowhere else to go as he boxed her in.

"Yeah." He leaned closer, resting a hand on either side of her. His nose brushed her cheek ever so faintly before he inhaled. She shivered.

His mouth pressed near the shell of her ear. "I can smell the desperation on you."

She swallowed the ball of emotion rising in her throat. She had to be strong. She had nowhere else to go. This man was nothing like the boy she'd left eight years ago. That Turner had been kind and caring. He'd been protective, and for one brief moment, she'd believed he'd really seen her. But she'd been wrong back then. Maybe this was the real Turner Walker.

She pressed her hand against his solid chest, but he didn't budge. "You better back off. As you know, I have no qualms about taking away your ability to spawn children."

His eyes flashed with what seemed like amusement and the corner of his mouth tilted up as if he wanted to smile. His lips thinned as he took two steps backwards.

"How long have you been here?" he asked.

She shrugged and took a breath, trying to calm her nerves. "A couple months."

His jaw clenched. "Seems like you're getting mighty cozy with my dad. Almost like you're a little family."

Maddy's gaze narrowed, and she crossed her arms. "Just what are you insinuating?"

"There you are." Gerry's voice drew their attention to the doorway. He had a very wiggly Josh by the hand. "Those lawns aren't going to mow themselves, T. And Aida wanted your input on a water fountain for her backyard. Be sure you stop by there first."

"I didn't think I'd be starting work today. I just got in, and you didn't even know I was coming early. Can't one of your other employees take care of it?" Turner asked.

"They've got enough on their schedule. Besides, idle hands are the devil's workshop," Gerry answered in a no-nonsense tone as his gaze darted between his son and Maddy.

"I'll go out with you today. But tomorrow, you're on your own." Gerry handed a baseball to Josh. "Be good for your mama today, son."

Turner bristled, his shoulders drawing up to his ears. *What is his problem? Why is he such an asshole now?*

"Mommy, can we play tag?" Josh asked while Gerry snapped at Turner to get going.

Maddy smiled at her son. "We can do that on my lunch break. Mommy has to do some work in the office, so you know what that means?"

"It means I get to use my special toys!" Josh walked over to the basket in the corner with his coloring book and a few toys reserved for her work time.

She got busy, entering expenses and recording income. By the time she wrapped up, it was time to feed Josh who had made it onto her lap. While she'd worked the last hour, he pulled up a cartoon on her phone.

"Okay, let's get you some lunch."

"Me want mac and cheese." He handed her phone over.

"Oh, do you, now?"

She ran her hands through his dark brown hair. Sometimes the reminder of his biological father was painful. But this was her little boy. Her heart embodied outside her chest. The first person to truly love her unconditionally.

She kissed his cheek. "Come on, little prince. Let's get your tummy fed."

Later that evening, after an awkward dinner, Gerry brought out an old Candy Land game for Josh. He was still too little to play the game the right way, but he liked to move the pieces around the colorful board. Gerry made voices for each piece and had her son giggling.

Maddy glanced towards the stairs where Turner had thankfully gone up to his room. It hadn't taken her long to move her things into the guest room with Josh. She'd shared her room with him since he'd been born, and she'd missed having him so close.

The old clock on the wall chimed, signaling eight o'clock.

"Alright, little prince, it's time for bed. Say goodnight to Papa Walker."

"But me playing," he argued.

"Listen to your mommy and we can play again tomorrow," Gerry promised as he picked up the game pieces.

Josh slipped his arms around the man's neck and Gerry hugged her son back. Emotion swelled in her chest at the sight. Josh released him and lifted his arms to her. She carried him up the stairs, his tired little body relaxing against her.

"Wait, Mommy. I hafta say nigh-night to TT too." Josh couldn't pronounce Turner's name completely, so he'd opted for the nickname.

She froze in the hallway. "I don't know if that's a good idea, sweetie. Turner is probably busy."

"I'm not." Turner's muffled voice sounded from the other side of his bedroom door.

She sighed and closed her eyes.

"Can I, Mommy?"

"Okay."

He wiggled out of her arms and ran to the door as it opened.

Maddy's shoulders tensed as her lips pursed. She could take Turner's wrath, but if he thought he could be a jerk to her son, he would find out just what this mama bear was made of.

Turner stood in the doorway, his hair still wet from his shower and slicked to the side. He bent down so he was eye level with her son. Her heart thudded against her rib cage as she held her breath.

Turner's face softened as he looked at her child. "Hey, bud, you going to bed?"

"Yeah. Nigh-night." Josh spread his little arms for a hug.

Her chest tightened. Would Turner reject him? "Remember to ask for hugs, sweetie."

Josh's hands were already wrapped around Turner's neck. The man's eyes flashed with surprise before he wrapped his big arms around her son's tiny body. Tears burned the back of

Maddy's eyes. She blinked them away as Josh pulled back with a smile.

"Sweet dreams, bud." Turner's voice was gravelly with emotion.

Maddy blinked in surprise. His gaze darted to hers and then any trace of softness disappeared, replaced with a steely glare.

"Come on, baby." She took Josh's hand and led him into the bedroom.

He snuggled in the bed, and she read him a story as his eyes fluttered closed. She kissed her son and slipped out of the room. Exhaustion crept up her tight shoulders. She rolled her head, stretching her neck before slipping into the bathroom to begin her routine for her second job.

She scrubbed her skin raw, shaved, and lotioned her body until she glowed with the shimmery dust the crowd seemed to love. Next, she curled her hair with the flat iron, finishing it off with hair spray. She teased it to give her that fresh-fucked look. Then, she applied more makeup than she'd usually wear, but the job called for it. She was putting on one of her many masks so that her son could have a better life.

By the time she was finished, hours had passed. She slipped out of the bathroom and knocked on Gerry's bedroom door.

"Come in."

She peeked in. "Hey. I'm heading out. Thanks for keeping an eye on him."

Gerry looked up from his novel. His reading glasses rested on his nose. "No problem. You know I love spending time with the little guy."

She smiled, gratitude glowing in her chest. He was the only man who was ever there for her when she needed him. Not even the people who shared her blood cared half as much. "I appreciate everything you're doing for us. I promise we'll be out of your hair as soon as possible."

He frowned. "I hope not. But I understand you'd want your own space. Just remember, my home is your home for as long as you want."

She blinked quickly, staving off the tears. "Have a good night, Gerry."

"You too, sweetheart. Be safe."

She nodded and closed the door behind her. She quickly tiptoed past Turner's closed door and slipped down the stairs. She reached for the door.

"Going somewhere?"

She jumped. *Turner.*

She pressed her hand over her racing heart. "Christ, you scared me!"

He stepped from the shadows of the low-lit kitchen. "Where are you going out so late? Leaving your kid here and dressing up like that to go party? What kind of a mother are you?"

The accusation stung. Maddy reared back as if he'd slapped her. Anger boiled over as her fists clenched. "I'm going to work. I'm not leaving my child because I want to, but because I don't have a choice."

His eyes flared with surprise as they dipped over the leggings and T-shirt she wore. Her work clothes were in her bag in the car. She tried to keep that life as separate from her son as possible. It was only temporary. She needed a lot of cash, fast. And it was best if no one could trace it back to her and find out her location. She didn't need anyone from her old life following her here to Shattered Cove.

"I didn't think you were the type to lie when you've clearly been caught."

She shrugged, acting like his venom didn't bother her.

"And I didn't think you were a bitter asshole who was the type to hold on to grudges, but here we are."

His jaw clenched as his eyes narrowed. "You didn't answer my question. Where are you going?"

Panic constricted her airways. There was no way in hell she was telling him and giving him even more ammunition to hate her, or look down on her. She was doing whatever she had to in order to give her son the best life she could. That's all that mattered. There was no shame in what profession she engaged in. But Turner would find a way to twist the knife into her already wounded side if he found out.

"None of your goddamned business." She brushed past him, but he caught her arm, halting her.

"This isn't your house, you can't go and come as you please and leave your kid here while you go off gallivanting."

She tore her arm free and leveled him with a glare. "Last I checked, this wasn't your house either."

His gaze darkened as his mouth twisted in what she assumed was disgust. Maddy left the house, hurrying to get the car started and get out of there before she lost her nerve. The man was infuriating. And if he found out where she was headed, her situation would be compromised and she might be forced to leave again. But where could she go when there was nowhere else to run?

4

TURNER

Turner fumed. The second her headlights left the driveway, he jumped into his car, backed out of the garage, and followed behind her at a safe distance.

Where are you going, princess? His father might be fooled by this innocent act, but he was not. Was she sneaking out to see her boyfriend? A sudden burning erupted in his chest. Turner rubbed a circle over his breastbone. It was probably heartburn from her cooking.

He grit his teeth as she pulled off the main road. The flashing neon sign for The Pearl Necklace glowed in the night sky.

Oh, this gets better and better. "She's a fucking stripper?" He shook his head in disbelief. No way. Surely not. He parked the car and walked up to the door. He'd been here before, back before he left for boot camp as a last hurrah with his friends. It seemed the place was under new ownership now.

He paid the cover to the burly bouncer by the door and walked in. Red dim lights cast the large room in an erotic shadow. A pulsing sexy beat reverberated through the speak-

22

ers. On the main stage to his right were two topless women gyrating on one another. On either side of them were large see-through cubes. Two women made out in one cube, while two men did the same in the opposite one. A little something for everyone it seemed.

Beyond the stage on either side were doors and a bouncer situated at each one. The one to the right led to private rooms for lap dances the last time he was here. But the one on the left was new.

He scanned the bar to his left. Black marble countertop gleamed in the overhead light. Two mixologists worked through the busy line.

"You gonna stand here staring all night, or do you want to buy a private dance?" a hostess asked, running her hand over his arm.

Turner shook it off. "I, uh, I'm just here for a drink," he muttered and walked to the corner of the bar.

He grabbed a seat one guy exited after being led away by a woman wearing a sexy nurse outfit and a red choker around her neck. Turner kept his gaze fixed to the pair as they walked up to the left of the stage. She said something to the bouncer and he waved a wand over the man, then pulled out a card reader from his pocket. A moment later they were waved through, disappearing behind a red curtain.

"What can I get you, sweetie?" the blonde behind the bar asked, batting her eyelashes at him. Two black X's covered her nipples, but other than that, she was completely topless.

"A Jack and Coke, please." He handed over a twenty.

She grabbed the cash with a smile and got to work mixing his liquor.

"You wouldn't happen to know when Maddy comes on, would you?"

She met his gaze, seeming to study him a little closer now. "Scarlett's on next."

His brows drew together as she set his drink in front of him and handed over the cash. Turner waved his hand. "Your tip."

She tucked the money in the thigh-highs under her micro miniskirt before she leaned in and nodded towards the stage. "Scarlett's on now."

He turned in his seat as the music changed to "I like it like that" by Cardi B.

Maddy stepped out onto the stage. Gone were the leggings and T-shirt she'd left in. They'd been replaced by sky-high black stripper heels and fishnet stockings that disappeared into a black leather skirt—if you could call it that. Turner's mouth went dry. The top of the stockings passed the strip of leather and ended below her belly button. A tiny diamond stud sparkled under the stage lights. They switched from red to strobe lights, flashing as her hips swayed with every step. A mesh crop top covered a black lace bra, contrasting against her pale skin. Her blond hair was teased and tousled like she'd just been fucked. Turner's cock jumped to attention as she licked her glossy bloodred lips and ran her hand down her neck over the black choker to her breasts. Her big blue eyes seemed almost unearthly highlighted in dark eye liner and shimmery shadow.

She gripped the pole and dropped, squatting on the ground, her thong peeking out from the strip of leather passing for a skirt. She twisted and turned, moving her body to the beat in a show designed to tease the most steadfast man. Turner fought the urge to run onto stage and carry her off over his shoulder. This was Maddy, but it wasn't. This woman knew how to work every part of her body to drive a man crazy. He tore his gaze from her. It seemed she'd garnered every other man's attention in the room too.

"Yeah, baby! Let me see those titties!" someone jeered.

Turner's hand fisted as his eyes darted back to Maddy. She bent low, arching her back, crawling over the stage, stopping to shake her ass. *Holy fuck.*

Maddy flipped upside down, supporting her weight with her arms as her legs opened wide into a split. Money rained down on the stage as she clapped her legs together and did it again. He was mesmerized, unable to look away even if his life depended on it. Maddy tipped her high heels over her head, nearly folding herself in half.

She straightened herself out and rolled to her belly, tipping her head back as she crawled across the stage, licking her lips and giving the front row *fuck me* eyes. That burning feeling returned to his chest with a vengeance. Turner tensed as Maddy got to her knees and spread her legs, flashing everyone her thong before standing. Her hands went to her hips as she shimmied them, slowly, sensually, slipping the skirt off her legs. She danced, turning around and giving everyone a flash of her juicy ass as she jiggled and twerked. She grabbed the pole, spinning around it before moving to the center of the stage once more. Next to go was the mesh shirt. More bills rained down on the stage. Shouts for her to bare it all rose. It seemed the whole room leaned towards her, captured in her erotic spell, hungry for whatever she'd give them. Turner hated that he, too, was entranced by her. He held his breath. Surely she wouldn't—

Maddy gripped the front clasp of her lace bra. She tossed a flirtatious smile to the crowd and spun around. The lace slipped from her shoulders as she gripped the pole, spinning and climbing higher before she bent backwards, flashing them her bare breasts.

Turner's body flashed with liquid heat. Lust and anger swirled inside him as she twisted herself around the pole, her breasts bouncing with her movements. She climbed higher, until she was two stories up, and then she let go, spinning so fast, he lurched to his feet. His chest tight, senses alert as her little body squeezed around the pole. She stopped right before the floor of the stage.

The song ended as a voice came over the speakers. "Give it up for Scarlett the harlot!"

The crowd cheered as Maddy picked up her clothes and blew everyone a kiss. Her eyes connected with his. She froze, her smile disappearing for a moment before it was back, big as ever, though she turned away and disappeared past the bouncer on the right of the stage.

"How do I get a private dance with her?" Turner turned to the bartender.

She smiled and nodded towards the place where Maddy had just disappeared. "Get in line."

Turner downed his drink with a wince and headed towards the literal line forming by the bouncer.

He had no choice but to wait as man after man entered the room. Minutes trickled by like hours until it was finally his turn. He handed over his credit card.

"Purple room. No touching if you want to keep your hands attached to your body." The bouncer gave him a look that would send a lesser man packing.

Turner nodded. "Got it."

He walked down the hall to the purple room and took a seat in the simple chair in the center of it. The walls matched the lilac door, as well as the lights. He took a deep breath and let it out. *What am I doing here?*

He was going to face her where she couldn't hide. Did his dad know what she was doing? No. He couldn't. What was she doing back in Shattered Cove? Why was she doing this, of all jobs? Never in a million years would he have imagined Maddy Miller, a daughter of one of the most prominent businessmen on the East Coast, would be taking her clothes off for money.

Music filtered in from the speakers overhead. Something with a heavy beat. Sensual bass vibrated through him as "She Bad" played in the room. The door opened and Maddy walked in wearing close to nothing, and shut the door before she looked up. Her eyes widened before her pouting red lips dropped open.

"W-what are you doing here?"

"I want a lap dance."

She blinked and looked down, a rosy hue tainting her cheeks. Surely this was all an act. There was no way a woman who could take her clothes off in front of a crowd of men would be embarrassed over this. But damn, she was good at acting.

She hesitated as if thinking it through a moment before she walked up to him, determination set in her gaze. "Sit back."

He leaned back, spreading his legs wide. This is where he should talk to her, confront her like he'd come in here to do. Maddy stepped closer, her chest rising and falling as if she were taking deep breaths. She only had the thigh-highs, her thong and lace bra on that left nothing hidden upon closer inspection.

Turner swallowed as her thigh brushed against his. Electricity sparked straight to his cock. His dick pressed against the teeth of his zipper as she whined her hips, dancing to the music. Maddy turned around, climbing backwards on him. Her hands fell to the floor, her thighs on either side of his, and her juicy ass front and center for his viewing pleasure as she jiggled.

"Fuck," he hissed.

She sat back up, wiggling on his hard cock. He tensed, fisting his hands. She was working him into a frenzy. That lace slipped off her shoulders once more, teasing him with her naked back. Her spine curved as she flipped over, straddling him. Her pink nipples made his mouth water. His hands itched to reach out and touch her.

Did she do this for my dad too?

His stomach lurched. Red-hot anger licked up his spine.

"Get off me," he said, anger lacing his tone.

Hurt flashed in her gaze as she froze. A moment later, she climbed off him, her eyes alight with fury. "You think you know who I am, but you have no idea."

"People don't change that much." She was a manipulative bitch in high school and it seemed that hadn't changed.

She turned for the door.

He stood to follow, grabbing her hand.

She slapped it away. "No touching."

"I paid for this time." He ground. He just needed some goddamned answers. What would make someone like her turn to this line of work? Things didn't add up.

She stopped, her body tensing before she shook her head and turned around. Her shoulders sunk in defeat. Gone was the anger and hurt in her expression, replaced with emptiness. Her expression was cold and lifeless as she returned to his lap. She moved around him, but it was different this time, like she wasn't really here.

He should be happy that he'd gotten to her. Instead, guilt gnawed at him. This woman stirred up so many emotions in him. She'd tormented his best friend, possibly seduced his father, and now she was engulfing him in a lust fire he'd never experienced. How could she wield so much power over him? His hands rested on her hips.

She slapped them away. "No touching."

"Oh, is that extra?"

She jerked off him, grabbing her bra off the floor. She turned to him, eyes glistening, sending a sword through his heart. "I'm not a whore."

"Could have fooled me," he scoffed.

She stepped closer, pointing her finger accusingly at him. "Keep your fucking money. You want more than a dance? Ask someone with a red choker. Otherwise, go fuck yourself." She ran out of the room, slamming the door behind her.

"Fuck!" he yelled and hung his head. That woman got under his skin like no one else. He looked down at his hands, shimmery with the same fine glitter that had painted her body. He winced. Why had he said those things to her?

Because I don't like how she makes me feel so out of control.

He'd been fooled by her innocent act once before. He wouldn't be made the fool again. And he wouldn't let his father fall into her trap either. He was going to expose her for the fake she was.

5

———————

MADDY

Maddy sipped her coffee and wiped her tired eyes. Memories from the night before flitted through her. Her stomach twisted in anxiety. She needed to get her and Josh away from Turner. His words had sliced through her, shredding what little confidence she could muster. Sure, she saw people from high school from time to time, but none of them had treated her like trash. She inhaled a shaky breath and forced the tears back. She would do whatever it took for her son and keep him safe from the ghosts of her past that never seemed to stop chasing her.

"Thank you, Maddy," Gerry said, and he took a mouthful of the pancakes she'd made at Josh's request. "I was thinking Josh and I could go fishing today. Maybe you could take a nap?"

"She wouldn't be needing a nap if she did honest work." Turner's steely voice cut through her.

Dread swirled in her gut as she plated a pancake for her son. "Here you go, baby."

"Mmmm." Josh's eyes rounded as he dug into his breakfast. "Fank you, Mama."

She kissed his head and grabbed her coffee before sitting at the table, avoiding looking at Turner.

"She does honest work," Gerry answered.

"Yeah? Do you know where she was last night?"

Maddy glared at him. *Don't you say a fucking thing in front of my son.*

Gerry stood abruptly, grabbing his son's ear and dragging him out the back door.

"Ow! Dad!"

Josh reached out for her arm, his eyes lighting with fear. "Is Papa Walker mad at TT?"

"He'll be alright. Eat your breakfast." She brought her untouched pancakes to the sink. She couldn't eat now. Gerry's and Turner's voices filtered in through the open screen.

"What the hell is wrong with you lately?" Gerry demanded.

"Do you know she's a stripper?" Turner growled.

Gerry sighed. "Did I raise a son to shame a woman for her choice of career or how she uses her body?"

"No, but—"

"But nothing. What do you think would drive a woman like Maddy to work at a place like that?"

Turner remained silent.

"I was that family's landscaper for years. I saw and heard things that girl went through that would make you feel ashamed you ever made her feel unwelcome even for a second," Gerry explained curtly.

Did he pity her? What did he know?

"For a smart man, you can be the biggest idiot. You better watch yourself and treat that woman with respect, or you can find another place to stay."

Maddy sucked in a sharp breath. Gerry was standing up for her at the risk of the relationship with his own son? Her heart lurched. Tears blurred her vision. Gratitude welled in her chest. Not even her own family had treated her half as kindly as the man out there.

But the last thing she wanted was to get between father and son. And she couldn't leave yet and risk homelessness and her son's safety. *I just need a little more time.*

Turner and Gerry returned to the kitchen as she slipped her plate into the dishwasher. "You know, I think Josh would love to go fishing," she said. "And I can help Turner out with the landscaping today."

"What?" Turner paled.

"Maddy, you need to rest," Gerry argued.

"No, it's fine. I could use the extra hours anyways." She forced a smile and hoped it looked genuine.

"You don't have to," Gerry assured her.

"I'd love to get my hands dirty. It's a nice day and everything." She tilted her head to the side as she crossed her arms across her chest. If this would earn her a drop of respect with Turner and make things easier for the men in the house, she'd do it for Gerry. The man had saved her more than once. "When do we leave?"

Five hours later, they were at their third location for the day. Maddy wiped the sweat from her brow. Her back was killing her. Every muscle ached. She hadn't gotten to soak in the tub after her dance last night. Usually, Epsom salts did wonders.

"Maddy Miller?"

She sat up, wincing at the pain radiating in her lower back that was almost as bad as the throbbing in her head.

"Oh my God. It is you! How are you, girl?" The overly

excited voice came from none other than Hayley, one of the girls in her friends circle from high school. The girl had followed her around and told everyone they were best friends. Maddy had played the part, she supposed, but as she'd learned that prom night, she hadn't had any real friends. Hayley was simply a girl who stayed in her shadow and copied everything Maddy did in the hope of getting some of the attention.

"Hey, Hayley. How are you?"

"Better than you it seems. It's nearly one hundred degrees. What are you doing out here melting in my parents' garden?"

Maddy lifted the clumps of weeds, hoping it was self-explanatory—though Hayley had never been an observant one.

Hayley gave an obnoxious high-pitched laugh as she waved her perfectly manicured hand on the air. "Wow, I never thought I'd see you back in Shattered Cove after . . . well, everything."

If Maddy's cheeks could grow any hotter, they would have.

"We should hang out and catch up. Oh, I know my brother would love to see you after all this time. He's single now. Maybe I could fix you up if you're looking?"

"I'm not paying you to gabber on. You're here to work," Turner snapped, interrupting their moment.

She shouldn't have felt relief, but she did.

"Oh, of course. Don't let me keep you." Hayley's sharp gaze roamed over Turner before a smile tipped her lips. "Turner, I didn't know you were back in town either. Seems like a reunion all of a sudden. You've certainly grown into a fine specimen." Hayley's gaze cut to Maddy's once more, mischief lighting her eyes.

Oh no.

"Maybe you had the right idea, slumming it with this guy

back in school. I'd get my hands dirty for a chance to sink my claws into that too." Hayley sneered before she waved goodbye and headed back to the Mercedes Bentz in the driveway.

Turner's jaw clenched.

"What's wrong? Don't like being objectified?" she joked.

He scoffed, cutting her a hard glare. "I don't like being reminded of how you fooled me before. Don't worry. It won't happen again." He turned to walk away.

Is that what he thought? I was never anything but honest with him in school. I showed him the real me. He's the one who believed the worst in me after everything.

"Turner—" She stood. The pounding in her head increased. Her empty stomach sloshed as the world spun around her. And then, everything went black.

6

———

TURNER

The anger seeped out of Turner's body the moment Maddy's body slumped to the ground. He ran over to her, rolled her to her back. Her face seemed so innocent with her eyes closed, so vulnerable. He pressed a hand to her flushed skin, Maddy was on fire. Damn. Why hadn't she told him she was so hot? She hadn't uttered one complaint all day. And he'd worked her hard. *I'm an asshole.* And now Maddy was in danger because of him.

Slipping one arm under her neck and the other beneath her knees, Turner picked her up. He needed to get her cooled off and hydrated quick. Lifting her into the truck, he laid her against the seat as she stirred. He put the air-conditioning on full blast before digging in the cooler for water and ice packs. Turner opened her door, sticking one frozen block behind her neck.

A small gasp left her lips as her eyes blinked open. Hazily, her gaze met his. "What—"

"When was the last time you drank some water?" He lifted

the bottle to her lips without waiting for an answer. She sipped it obediently.

"Did you eat breakfast?" he asked. Not enough water in this heat could be deadly. Add onto that her lack of sleep last night and possible low blood sugar, and she might need to go to the hospital.

"Not really." Her voice was soft.

He took her hat off and rubbed the sweaty hair from her head. Her vulnerable blue gaze met his. "I'm sorry."

She was apologizing to him? "I'm the one who owes you an apology."

Her eyes widened.

Yeah, he'd been the worst kind of asshole to her. He'd thought she wasn't able to work hard, but she was. And everything his dad had said—he was right. Maddy was doing what she had to for her son. That was the most important thing. "I'm sorry. I shouldn't have said the things I did to you."

"Thank you."

He handed her the water bottle. "Drink all of this. Not too fast. And eat the granola bar in the console. I'll pack up and we'll call it a day."

He shut the door before she could respond and gathered their tools and supplies before climbing back in the truck. She was already asleep.

He drove to the grocery store, parking in the shade. He'd planned to slip out but she blinked her eyes open.

"Just running in for a couple things for dinner. Be right back."

"Oh, I have to get some stuff, too, while we're here. If you don't mind?" She reached for the door handle.

"Suit yourself." He climbed out of the car and walked over to her side. The last thing he wanted was for her to pass out on the asphalt and really hurt herself. He slipped his hand to her lower back.

"I'm okay. I won't faint again." Her back stiffened.

He dropped his palm, but stayed near her until they walked into the air-conditioned store. The cool air hit him like a blast from the freezer section compared to the humidity outside.

She grabbed a basket and took off to one side of the store, so he did the same in the opposite direction. When he was finished, he got in line behind her.

The cashier rang her up, and Turner took the time to really study her. Several strands of her sweat-soaked hair stuck to her neck. She moved as if every muscle in her body was tense and sore. *Because she spent the night dancing and then I made her do physical labor.* Being hunched over the flower beds and weeding was not an easy task, especially in the hundred-degree weather. Her back was probably killing her. Dark circles had formed under her eyes like bruises. Had she gotten any sleep last night?

Her gaze flicked to his as her sun-kissed cheeks reddened even more. "I'll put back the ice cream." She spoke to the cashier, a bored-looking teenage boy.

"Without it, your total comes to nineteen-fifty." The boy nodded to the twenty-dollar bill in her hand.

"I got it." Turner opened his wallet.

"No." She shook her head, the red in her cheeks deepening. "It's fine."

The boy looked between her and him.

"Just take it. I owe you for today anyways." Turner pushed the ten-dollar bill towards her.

Her jaw clenched as she looked around at the few stares they'd drawn from the elder lady behind them and the couple perusing flowers to the right of the register. She shook her head. "I don't need your help," Maddy hissed, then turned her glare onto the cashier.

He set the frozen treat aside and finished cashing her out. Maddy took her bags and walked out of the store without giving him a second glance.

Turner sighed and moved farther down the checkout lane. "Add the ice cream to my stuff."

Maddy was asleep when he returned to the truck—or at least she pretended to be. He drove them home. As soon as the key was out of the ignition, she bolted from the car.

He met her in the kitchen and set the ice cream on the counter. "I was only trying to help."

Her shoulders climbed to her ears before she left the room without a word. Turner put away the rest of the groceries, sticking the frozen treat in the freezer.

Maddy slammed down a few bills on the counter in front of him. "Here."

His brows drew together. "I told you I owe you for today."

"And I'll get that on payday just like any other employee. I won't take your pity." She spun around and left the room before he could protest. The water in the bathroom turned on.

Half an hour later, he was freshly showered and crept downstairs past her room. She was probably sleeping after the ordeal she'd been through.

Turner went to the kitchen for a cold beer. Maddy was at the counter with Josh. She was in a pair of leggings that hugged her like a second skin and a T-shirt with a few holes in it, giving him a peek of her delicate skin underneath. The scene made his chest tight. She tossed a piece of shredded cheese into Josh's mouth and he giggled before giving her a kiss on the cheek. How was she still going? She must feel like a zombie.

Her tired eyes sparkled whenever she looked at her son. *What do you think would drive a woman like Maddy to work at a place like that?* His father's words came back to haunt him. *I saw and heard things that girl went through that would make you feel ashamed you ever made her feel unwelcome even for a second.* The weight of his actions hit him like a ton of bricks. How could he have let decades-old anger cloud his judgment so completely?

Maddy smiled again, her face lit up, and he knew.

Because she broke my heart.

"Can I help with dinner?" Turner asked.

Maddy's shoulders stiffened as she shook her head, not bothering to look at him.

"Mommy's making mac and cheese." Josh smiled excitedly.

"Sounds good. My mom used to make that too."

"Where is your mommy?" Josh asked.

"Bud, let's leave Turner alone," Maddy said as she sprinkled the last of the cheese over the dish.

Guilt sloshed in his gut. He popped the tab on his beer and gave a smile to the little guy. "It's okay. My mom died a long time ago."

Maddy bent over and slipped the casserole into the oven. His gaze dropped to her ass, and his cock twitched in his basketball shorts. *Down, boy.*

She stood and he quickly averted his eyes to Josh, whose eyes had gone glassy and wide. His little lip puckered out. *Oh, shit.*

"I don't want Mommy to die."

Maddy wrapped her arms around her son. "I won't, baby. I'm right here. I'm never leaving you."

"But TT's mommy died. What if you do?" Fat tears dripped down his little face, tearing Turner's heart in two.

Turner chugged half of his beer. *I just can't stop putting my foot in my mouth.*

"What if that mean man comes back?" Josh asked.

"He won't, baby," Maddy said, cradling her son as she carried him out of the room.

What mean man was Josh talking about? Was Maddy running from someone? Was she in danger?

7
____

MADDY

Maddy blinked her eyes open. The sun was up, which meant Josh had slept in. She turned on her side, reaching out her arm for him. Her hand met only cold sheets. She jolted upright and winced. Her back was still sore from all the work she'd done that weekend. *Where is Josh?*

She got out of bed and quickly stripped out of her sleep clothes and slipped on a fresh pair of undergarments, jean cutoffs, and one of her faded T-shirts. She pulled her hair into a messy bun as she walked down the stairs, searching for any sign of her son. The house was quiet. Too quiet. A slip of paper caught her attention on the coffee maker.

Gone golfing for the day. I won't be home for dinner, so don't wait up. -G

If Gerry was gone, then where was Josh? Panic constricted her lungs. She searched frantically as she ran through the house.

"Josh? Josh!"

The house was empty. *Oh, God. What if he'd gone outside? The road! What if someone had taken him? Or he'd wandered off? It's not like Josh to disappear like this.*

She bolted out the door, her heart beating out of her chest. A clamoring sound drew her attention to the garage. She ran in and stopped dead in her tracks. Her shoulders fell in relief. Her little boy stood on a milk crate next to Turner. Their attention was fixed on the lawn mower's engine.

"See, now we have to tighten this back up." Turner wrapped his big hand around her son's, letting the little boy be a part of whatever he was doing.

The action pulled at her heartstrings. Damn, if it didn't make the asshole hotter.

"Josh."

Turner and Josh both turned to her.

Josh's face split in a smile. "Mommy, look what TT is showing me. Me fix the tractor!"

She forced a smile and flicked her gaze towards Turner. "Thank you for, uh, watching him. He's not supposed to leave the house without me. I don't know how I didn't hear him get up this morning. Sorry if he bothered you." She reached out for Josh's hand, and he took it.

"He wasn't a bother. He's my big helper, right, bud?"

Josh's eyes lit up as he nodded. "Wight!"

She led her son off the makeshift stool as Turner wiped his hands on an old rag. "Can I talk to you for a minute?"

She cast a glance at her son. "Josh, why don't you kick the soccer ball around over there on the grass?"

Josh clapped his hands. "Watch me, otay? I make a big goal!" He ran off at full speed towards the little net Gerry had pulled out of storage for him.

Maddy crossed her arms and straightened her spine, preparing herself for whatever Turner was going to throw at her next.

"Maddy, I'm sorry. I treated you like shit and I could give you the excuse that I'm dealing with some personal stuff and seeing you brought a lot up for me from the past, but that's no excuse for me to treat you the way I have."

She turned towards him, her brows drawn up. He'd said as much yesterday, but she'd thought he just felt sorry for her after her fainting episode. Was this all an elaborate trick? "I'm still unclear as to why you would hate me so much."

He blew out a breath and stuck his hands in his pockets self-consciously. "Are you . . . dating my dad?"

Her gaze narrowed. "What?"

"I thought—I don't know. It made sense when I first got here. Why else would you be at my dad's house, of all places? I thought maybe Josh was his."

Her mouth dropped open. Of all the idiotic things this man could think. "You think I fucked a man old enough to be my father?"

He swallowed and looked at the ground like he was ashamed. He should be.

"Christ, tell me what you really think of me," she dead-panned. "And your dad. Don't you think he would have told you if he'd had another child?"

"I know. I fucked up. I want to make it up to you."

She snorted and turned back to Josh who was kicking the ball closer to the goalpost. "How could you do that?"

"You tell me." He stepped closer. His gaze made the fine hairs on the back of her neck stand up.

She turned towards him. His pale blue eyes locked on hers. He tipped his head slightly to the side, his sharp jaw creating a shadow on his neck. His Adam's apple bobbed as he swallowed. Her gaze flicked back to his, and she was sucked into those cloudy orbs like she'd been so many years ago. Back when they'd promised safety and the chance for something more, something real. Could she trust him not to abandon her when she needed him most?

No. She couldn't trust anyone. *Except Gerry.*

"Be kind to my son and cordial with me. I won't stay longer than absolutely necessary for Josh. I'll be out of your hair as soon as I can."

He reached out to her elbow. Sparks and shimmers of energy zinged up her arm. She gasped as his gaze widened. "I would never be mean to a child."

She pulled her arm away. "Well, I don't know that, do I? I don't assume you're the same person that you were in high school. The same one that helped me and made me feel…" *Seen. Safe.* "I'm not the same naive girl I was in high school and I don't assume you stayed the same either."

After a beat of silence, Turner rubbed the back of his neck and sighed. "So what you're saying is, we need to start over and get to know each other again?"

She shrugged. "Something like that."

"Okay." He turned towards her son who'd just scored a goal and was jumping up and down. "Josh, go inside and wash your hands. We're gonna go out to breakfast."

"What?" she asked. Her attention snapped back to the man at her side as Josh screamed, "Yay!" and ran inside.

"I never agreed to this."

"You said I needed to get to know the new you. That means we should spend some time together, no?" He gave her a flirty smile.

How had he turned this around on her? This was the charming Turner she remembered. The same one who'd convinced her that maybe someone could know the real her and love her back . . . and then he'd betrayed her like everyone else. And what was his goal here? Did he have an ulterior motive for trying to get closer to her? Did he want to dig up dirt on her so Gerry would kick her out? Did he just want to fuck her?

She sighed. She wasn't so sure she was ready to let this man back into her life. But that would make her a hypocrite, guilty of the same things she accused him of. So . . . she was going out to breakfast with Turner Walker.

8

TURNER

Turner sipped his iced coffee, peeking over Josh's shoulder. The little boy's tongue poked out the side of his mouth in concentration as he scribbled the red crayon all over the diner's coloring sheet.

"Looks like you're working hard over there," Turner said.

Josh stopped coloring long enough to look up at him, his little chest puffed out and his eyes glittering with pride. "Me making a red whale."

"I see that." Turner chuckled.

Josh's eyes fell on his chest. "One of my action figures has those. Mommy said they're doggy tags."

Turner flicked a glance at Maddy, who absently stirred her soda with the straw, before turning back to the kid. "Yup, they're dog tags. I was in the Navy."

"You were a soldier?" Josh's eyes rounded.

"We usually go by sailor, but yes."

"Did you get to travel?" Maddy asked. It was the first time she'd spoken directly to him since he'd announced they were going to breakfast.

He leaned back in the booth and centered the coffee cup in front of him before meeting her eyes. "Yeah. I was stationed in South Korea and then in Spain. So, on leave, I got to explore some of the surrounding countries too."

She smiled thoughtfully. "You always did want to see the world."

Her comment thrust him back in time, before everything went to hell in a handbasket.

Turner made his way to the stadium. He'd get a little more practice in before he went home. As he turned around the corner, a sniffle made him stop short. He spun around. A lone figure, curled in on herself, sat on the top bleacher.

What was Maddy Miller doing here? Was she crying? The popular queen bee had never shown an ounce of actual emotion in all the years he'd known her. She was always perfectly put together with a plastic smile or a sneer when she'd bullied those lower on the food chain.

Turner should keep walking. Maddy had targeted his own best friend, Jasmine. He shouldn't care if the girl had a heart or not . . . but he did.

He set down his gear in the grass and stepped up the bleacher stairs. She jolted upright, quickly wiping her eyes as if she were trying to hide the fact that she wasn't made of stone.

Her red puffy eyes hardened and narrowed on him. "What do you want?"

The crack in her voice tore at his heart. He sat beside her, leaving a few inches between them. He stared at the stadium, resting his feet on the metal bench below. "You okay?"

"What do you care?" she snapped.

Why did he? He shrugged. "Somebody ought to. And I'm the only one around."

She was silent for a beat. A bird flew overhead, alone, and Maddy tracked its progress as it soared over the field. She sighed defeatedly. "Do you ever wish you could just get out of here?"

He chuckled. "All the time."

"Where would you go?"

"Europe, Africa, and maybe Asia," he answered without having to think too hard on it. "What about you?"

"Anywhere but here . . . maybe France. I've always wanted to see the Eiffel Tower. Or the ruins in Rome and Greece."

He turned to her. "You like architecture or the history of those places?"

A faint smile shifted her lips—not the plastic one she gave everyone else, but a genuine display of happiness. His heart raced like he'd done that workout after all. He wanted to see what other emotions he could illicit from her.

"You'll think I'm stupid." She crossed her arms and shook her head dismissively.

"No, I won't."

"Promise?"

The flash of vulnerability in her sky-blue orbs stuttered his breathing. Where had this girl been during the last three and a half years of high school? He slashed his finger in an X over his chest. "Swear."

A slight blush rose to her cheeks and he leaned in, ready to hang on every word. She was gorgeous. The makeup she wore every day that was usually done to perfection was now smudged under her long eyelashes. It made her seem more human and not like the doll who walked the halls with her nose in the air. She wouldn't be caught dead talking to a boy whose father ran a landscaping company. Usually she hung out with the other rich kids with trust funds.

"I like the magic of those places," she said, a faraway, dreamy look in her eyes. "Paris is the city of love and romance. Hope. The ruins represent a past full of danger and mystery. It would be amazing to share the same space that who knows how many others had and imagine how it was back then. The competitions and the games." She opened her mouth and closed it as if she wanted to say more but didn't dare to. Her gaze dropped, and she tucked a piece of hair behind her ear. "It's stupid."

He reached out and grabbed her wrist. Lightning striking would have been less of a shock. She gasped, her eyes wide as she stared at him. Energy thrummed in his veins as he leaned closer, his eyes locked on hers.

"It's not stupid. You should go one day and see them all."

She licked her pink lips, making them shiny. Would they taste as sweet as she smelled?

"Turner?" Maddy's voice brought him back to the moment.

"Yeah?"

"Where'd you go?" Her brows drew together.

Back to before. He shook his head. "Sorry, just thinking."

"Here you go," Brynn, the waitress, said, setting their breakfast feast in front of them. Pancakes with bacon for Josh, the works for Turner, and a simple omelette and turkey sausage for Maddy.

"Thank you." Maddy smiled up at the woman.

"You're welcome. I'll be back in a while to check on you." Brynn left.

"Did you ever do any traveling?" Turner asked, digging into his eggs and home fries.

Maddy's shoulders curved inward before she reached for Josh's plate, cutting his meal up and drizzling maple syrup on his pancakes. She set the dish back in front of him.

"Not really," she said as her son dove into his food.

"Where were you living before you came here?" Turner asked, taking a sip of his now warm coffee.

She pushed the food around on her plate, not actually eating anything. "New York. Not the city—just another small town."

"What—"

Maddy stood abruptly. "I'm gonna use the restroom. Come on, Josh."

"But, Mommy, me eating panny-cakes," Josh protested.

"He can stay here with me," Turner offered.

Maddy nodded. "I'll be right back." She turned and walked to the back of the diner, then disappeared through the bathroom doors.

"Can I have some of your bacon?" Josh asked.

Turner surveyed their plates. Sure enough, the kid had consumed all of his own. "Sure. Help yourself."

Josh's chubby little hand reached out and snatched a piece from his plate. "Mmm. Bacon is my favorite."

Turner chuckled. "Me too, buddy."

"TT?"

"Yeah?"

"Can I live with you and Papa Walker forever?" Josh asked, his eyes rounding like a little puppy dog.

Turner angled his body so he could face him better. "What do you like about my dad's house so much?"

"Papa Walker is nice to me and Mommy. And you're a soldier, so you can keep us safe from the mean man and the monsters."

Turner's heart raced in his chest. This was the second time the kid had mentioned a mean man. What had he seen? He wanted to ask the boy, but this was a conversation that he should have with his mother. And he would get to the bottom of it as soon as he got her alone again.

He lifted his last piece of bacon and handed it to Josh. "I'll keep you safe, little man."

Josh stood on the booth seat and wrapped his arms around Turner's neck. "Fank you, TT."

He gently patted his tiny back. Josh was sweet—and he was beginning to care for him deeply.

Who would want to hurt him?

What if the mean man was Josh's dad?

What if he'd hurt Maddy?

Anger sloshed in Turner's gut and welled in his veins. If someone was trying to hurt Maddy and her son, they'd have to get through him first.

9

MADDY

Maddy cut open the bag of mulch and spread handfuls of it around the flowers she'd just planted. A water bottle appeared in front of her.

"Take a break and hydrate." Turner waved the bottle closer to her hand.

She pulled off her work gloves and accepted the drink from him, unscrewing the top and draining half of the icy liquid.

She handed it back to him, but he waved her off and sat beside her. She was working in the shade today, thankfully, but it was still hot. He'd taken the other side of the house, where the sun hit directly. *How sweet of him.* The kind gesture brought a flutter to her stomach. She wasn't used to being taken care of.

He wiped the trickle of sweat from his brow with his already mostly soaked shirt. He should just take it off. She licked her salty lips and averted her gaze. The last thing she needed right now was to be attracted to this man. Attraction to Turner never seemed to work in her favor.

"Can I ask you something?" Turner faced her.

She took another sip of water, buying herself some time. "I guess."

"Josh said something the other day."

Oh, God. What did he say? Worry cinched her gut. Kids had no filter.

"He asked me if I'd keep him safe from the mean man."

She took a deliberate slow, deep breath and let it out.

"Are you in danger?"

Maybe. When am I not running from something? "Before we moved back, our apartment was broken into."

Turner tensed. His body went rigid.

She kept her gaze focused on the label of the water bottle. She started peeling it off. "He tried to . . . hurt me . . . and well, we got away." *Are you going to pity me now? Or think I'm a bad mother?*

"Why go to my dad's?" Turner asked.

"I . . . I just needed somewhere to land until I could get back on my feet. Somewhere Josh would be safe. And I tried to think back to the last time I felt that way. He was the one who saved me on prom night when—" *Oh, shit.*

"When what?" Turner's attention burned the side of her face.

Her chest constricted with panic. Her eyes searched the yard, wildly seeking an escape. A heavy weight settled on her shoulders. Her breathing grew ragged. *He can't know. No one can know.*

"Maddy?" Turner's voice morphed as if she were in a wind tunnel.

Maddy was thrust back into that night.

Maddy's heart raced. A sick feeling twisted her gut as her prom date led her to the limo. Maybe she should find another way home.

"Come on, baby. I got a surprise for you." Brett tugged her hand hard, making her stumble. She hadn't even realized she'd stopped walking.

Don't be rude. Don't make a scene. *Her mother's words had been repeated millions of times over the course of her life. Maddy just needed to get to their next destination, an after-party, and all would be well. She could drink and dance with her friends. Maybe she'd get lucky and Brett would find someone else to take home tonight. Because she was not having sex with him. There was only one boy she wanted to lose her virginity to, but after that scene earlier, he might not forgive her. Surely, he must know she hadn't meant it.*

Brett opened the door for her and slipped his hands to her waist as she got in the limo. His cousin, Chris, had sat in the opposite side, hands outstretched, casually smoking a cigar, his legs spread wide like he owned the goddamned world. She'd never liked him. He made her skin clammy and her stomach knot. But he was Brett's older cousin and the son of her father's employer. So she did what she'd been trained to do—she sat there and did her best to be polite and look pretty. A doll set on the shelf. Only another month of this and she would be free.

The door to the limo clicked shut with finality. Chris knocked on the window separating the driver from them before the limo started to move.

"Here, have a drink." Brett handed her a glass of amber liquid.

There was no way she would drink anything from either of them— not after what she'd witnessed earlier. But she didn't want to make them angry. So, she lifted the liquor to her lips and pretended to take a sip, even throwing a fake wince in to make her performance believable. She set the drink down in one of the cup holders.

Brett kissed her cheek, his strong expensive cologne burning her nose. She turned her head away, trying to take an untainted breath. His mouth landed on her neck, placing sloppy kisses on her skin. How much longer until we're at the after-party? *Brett's hand drifted up her leg to her thigh, raising her dress.*

She slapped her hand down on his to stop the ascent. "Stop."

Brett gave one of his playful smiles. "Come on, stop being a tease.

I've waited long enough." He kissed her neck, his fingers digging into the soft flesh of her inner leg.

She tried to push his hand away, but it didn't budge. "Your cousin is here. Save that for later." There wouldn't be a later, but he didn't need to know that. She'd make her escape at the after-party.

"It's fine. He likes to watch." Brett sucked hard on her neck. She squirmed away. She didn't want any of his marks left on her.

"I like to do more than watch." Chris's voice was colder than she'd ever heard it. Her eyes widened, fear strangling her. Alarms blared. She needed to get out of the limo. She needed to get to safety.

"Stop. I don't want to do this."

Inky, dark arousal sparked in Chris's eyes as he crossed over to sit on the other side of her. His hand fisted the back of her hair, sending pain shooting over her scalp. She hissed, tears pricking the corner of her eyes.

"Please stop."

"God, I love it when they beg. Don't you, Brett?" Chris's voice grew ragged.

"I don't want this," Maddy cried.

"You shouldn't have interfered with our game earlier, then. Now you'll have to do."

Her stomach churned. Slipping a roofie to another girl was not a game. "Stop the car and let me out."

"Or what?" Brett asked, sliding his hand under her panties.

"Driver! HELP! Stop the car!" she screamed.

The guys laughed. "We've already given him a lump sum to do his job and drive without asking questions. The limo is as soundproof as they come, courtesy of my father. You can scream all you want, you little slut. No one will hear you. And no one will save you. You're at my mercy now." Chris pulled her hair hard so that she had no choice but to look up into his empty soulless eyes. "You wanna live? You do what I say."

She'd never felt more powerless nor terrified in her life.

"Now, suck Brett's cock while I fuck you like the little whore you are," Chris ordered. Oh, God. No! Nononono. This isn't happen-

ing. *Brett tore at her dress, exposing her breasts. Her mind searched frantically for a way out. But there was none. She was alone, trapped. No one would save her. She just had to survive.*

"Maddy!" Turner's voice ripped her out of the flashback. He was shaking her, or was she just trembling that hard?

"Maddy, come back to me." Turner rocked her back and forth in his arms. Hot tears spilled down her cheeks. Embarrassment flooded over her; the shame of that night was so thick it strangled her. A sob broke free as she pulled away.

He only held her tighter. "Shhhh, I'm here. You're safe. I got you."

She cried until she couldn't breathe.

"Come on, take a deep breath," he said, his eyes pleading with her until she nodded. "In—one, two, three, four—and out—one, two, three, four." He guided her through the deep-breathing exercises. She hiccuped and relaxed into his embrace, soaking it up because if he ever found out, he'd never look at her the same.

"What do you smell?" Turner asked.

She blinked, surprised at his question. "You?"

He chuckled. "Sorry about that."

He had nothing to be sorry about. Yes, he was sweaty, but he didn't stink. His masculine musk mixed with the sweet scent of earth was intoxicating.

"What do you see?"

Oh, so this is what we're doing. "The grass."

"Feel?"

"Your heartbeat." It was racing almost as fast as hers.

"Hear?"

"The baby birds in the nest in the tree above us." He was grounding her, connecting her back to her body.

"And taste?"

She licked her lips. "My tears."

He rubbed lazy circles over her back until her breathing normalized. "Do you want to talk about it?"

She shook her head, clamping her eyes closed.

"Okay." He stayed there, holding her like nothing else mattered. Like she meant something.

"Turner?"

"Yeah, princess?" The nickname sounded more like an endearment than it had the last time he'd used it.

"Thank you."

He didn't answer. Instead, he leaned down and kissed her forehead.

It was the gentle act of kindness that did her in. He was still the boy who saw *her*. But she was no longer the girl who believed in magic. If he looked closely enough, he'd see that she wasn't worthy of him anymore—or maybe she never had been. She pulled away from him, sitting on the grass.

"Why don't we call it a day and get pizza delivered for dinner so no one has to cook?" he asked.

She nodded, wiping her eyes. "I'd like that."

He reached out his hand to help her up, and he didn't let go all the way home.

10

TURNER

Turner pulled his shirt over his head and walked out of his room.

"Oof." Maddy thudded against his chest.

He reached out to steady her. "Sorry. Wasn't watching where I was going."

She gave him a tentative smile but didn't meet his gaze. She pulled away and nodded. "I'm going to lie down for a few minutes."

He opened his mouth to say something, but she'd already disappeared into her room. It had been days since she'd broken down in his arms. She hadn't said much, nor been able to meet his eyes since. He sighed and headed down the stairs.

His phone vibrated in his back pocket. Turner pulled it out, a rock forming in the pit of his stomach as Stephanie's name flashed on the screen. He clicked to open the message.

Steph: *Hey, just wanted to give you an update. Everything should be in order for us to move forward soon. The lawyers are going over the paperwork. I'll come to town and we can meet for dinner. I'd love to see your dad again too. Miss you. Xoxo.*

He cast a quick glance up the stairs and then tapped out a reply.

Turner: *Sounds good. Let me know when you're coming. The Lighthouse Inn has some nice rooms on the beach.*

He tucked his phone back in his pocket. Usually, she'd stay here at his dad's with him, but that wouldn't work with Maddy and her son here.

Turner grabbed a bottle of water and headed out the back door. Josh was running through the sprinkler as his father watched on with a smile on his face and a squirt gun in his hand.

"You seem to be enjoying retirement." Turner sat on the patio chair, crossing his ankle over his knee.

His father chuckled. "More than I thought I would. You finish the McCray property today?"

"Yup."

His dad nodded.

Turner took a sip of water as Josh clamped his hand over one of the sprays of water, giggling. "Maddy said something to me the other day."

"Yeah?"

Turner leaned forward so he didn't need to speak as loud. "She told me you saved her on prom night."

His father's eyes darkened as his arms flexed with tension, his body going rigid before he took a deep breath. "It's not my story to tell, son."

But there was a story there. And from the looks of his father's reaction, it wasn't one Turner was going to like hearing.

"But I can tell you that out of everyone she knew, all her so-called friends and family, she called *me*, the family landscaper. That should say something."

Turner's stomach twisted and knotted. *What happened to her?* He tried to think back to that night. Finding her and her date,

Brett, and his cousin, Chris, who was far too old to be at prom. Hayley had been with them too, practically salivating off the man's arm. They were in front of Jasmine, laughing.

Turner ran up to them as Maddy sneered at Jasmine. "Serves you right for thinking a slut like you had the right to talk to us. Run on home now. No one wants to get herpes tonight, skank."

Turner saw red. Anger swelled like a red tidal wave. How could Maddy be so vile? "What the fuck is your problem!"

Maddy's ice-blue eyes turned towards him, panic streaking through her features as her cheeks bloomed pink. She almost looked like she regretted it. The guys next to her laughed.

She flicked a glance their way and then back to him before those orbs turned steely. Like she'd slipped on a mask. The haughty expression was back.

She flipped her hair over her shoulder and rolled her eyes. "She's a walking epidemic. She probably has AIDS too."

Jasmine trembled against him, but remained quiet, which meant Maddy had probably gutted her. Usually Jasmine was vocal and gave it right back to the spoiled princess.

Turner tightened his hold on Jasmine and shook his head at Maddy. "You must really hate yourself if you have to treat someone as wonderful as Jaz like this."

Maddy gave a pitiful laugh, but her armor cracked just enough for him to glimpse the sorrow in her guarded eyes. He turned and led Jasmine away from them, opting to ditch the rest of prom and bring her spirits up.

Later that night, as Jasmine giggled next to him by the hordes of toilet paper they'd gathered to TP the neighborhood, his phone rang in his pocket. Pulling it out, fury swirled in his chest. Why the fuck was Maddy calling him? Did she really think he could forgive her after that? She wasn't who he'd thought. And he wouldn't make the same mistake again and fall for the mistress of manipulation. She'd shown her true colors tonight.

Turner's chest squeezed tight. *Maddy called me that night and*

I didn't answer. How could she have expected him to after what she'd said to his best friend? It must have been bad if she'd called his dad and not her parents. Had someone hurt her?

The way she'd broken down in his arms the other day was the realest he'd ever seen her. Everything inside him screamed at him to protect her. Whoever Maddy was, she'd changed. Right? Maybe that night changed her. Or the years since then.

He couldn't help the niggling voice in his head telling him this was all an elaborate manipulation for her to get what she wanted. But what could he or his dad possibly offer her?

11

MADDY

Maddy leaned against the bookshelf as Josh listened intently to the drag queen, Miss Marsha Divine, as she entertained the kids with her elaborate costume and sparkly makeup. As soon as she'd heard of the local bookstore offering a drag queen story hour, she'd marked it on her calendar. She wanted Josh exposed to people from all walks of life so that he could have more empathy and understanding. So far removed from how she'd been.

A little girl in the front raised her hand.

"Yes, Zoey?" Marsha asked.

"Are you a boy or a girl?"

Marsha smiled and leaned down so that she was eye level with the children. "I am a boy, but I love to dress up and wear makeup. When I'm performing in drag, I love to be called a girl, or she/her. When I'm not dressed up, I go by boy pronouns. Do you know what pronouns are?"

Zoey nodded her head. "Yes, Mommy told me I'm she and my brother is a he but some people are not either and we call them they."

"Your mommy is a smart cookie, just like you." Marsha took a seat on the chair behind her and pulled out a book. "Okay, who's ready for the story?"

A collective, "Me!" was shouted by the group of kids that had gathered.

Maddy had kept to the back of the wall of other parents. She searched their faces. Would she recognize any of them from school? She tucked a piece of hair behind her ear as nerves swam in her belly. She had so many past sins to atone for.

"Excuse me." A feminine voice pulled her attention from behind her.

Maddy straightened and moved away from the bookshelf. "Sorry."

"Oh, don't be. I just needed to grab this one." The woman bounced a baby in the carrier across her chest as she picked a novel from the shelf before turning to her with a smile that quickly dimmed.

Jasmine.

Jasmine's jaw slackened as her eyes rounded.

Maddy tried to offer her a friendly smile. "Hey."

"Madeline?" Jasmine patted her hand on the back of the baby as she inched away from her.

"Yeah. I'm back in town." *And I'm sorry.* How could she begin to apologize?

Jasmine's gaze cut to the kids and back to her. "You here for story hour?"

Maddy nodded and stuck her hands in her pocket. "Yeah, I wanted to bring Josh, my son."

"You're a mom?"

Maddy winced. "I know. Who would have thought, right?"

Jasmine didn't smile.

"I owe you a big apology. A lot of them, actually."

Jasmine's eyebrows drew together in disbelief.

"I was a bitch to you in high school and I can't tell you how sorry I am. I wondered if maybe, you'd be willing to hear me out?"

Jasmine shook her head.

Maddy's heart sank. "I understand."

"No. I don't think you do." A curious smile turned Jasmine's lips upward. "I just can't believe Madeline Miller is standing in front of me, wearing something off-brand, not a stitch of makeup and apologizing to me, messy mom bun and all."

Maddy swallowed and forced a laugh as she looked to the floor. "I'm not that girl anymore."

"I can see that."

Maddy met her gaze.

Jasmine offered her a tentative smile. "After this, we could walk over to Green Park? My daughter and your son can play while we chat? I think this little guy will be up soon for a feeding anyways."

Maddy nodded. "I'd like that. Which one is yours?"

Jasmine pointed out the little girl with jet-black hair who'd asked the question. "That's Zoey."

"I don't know how I didn't see it before. She looks a lot like you." *Except for those grey eyes.*

Jasmine smiled, a little bit of pain mixed with her pride. "She does."

After story time concluded, Maddy followed Jasmine to the park. Zoey held Josh's hand as she excitedly babbled on about *Paw Patrol* and *Daniel Tiger*. Josh stared at her in awe, his adorable smile never leaving his face.

They set up in the sand box, Zoey directing him on how to build a proper fairy house and Josh happily doing her bidding.

"How old is she?" Maddy asked as she settled onto the bench.

Jasmine took the spot next to her. "She's five and a half. Hart is seven months." The little boy wiggled in the carrier, whimpering. Jasmine loosened the strap of the carrier and pulled her shirt up, offering the baby her breast.

Maddy turned towards the kids, giving Jasmine some privacy as she nursed her son.

"And Josh?" Jasmine asked.

"Three."

"He's adorable," Jasmine mused.

"Thank you." Maddy turned to face Jasmine, still able to see her son out of the corner of her eye. But what she had to say required eye contact. "I haven't told anyone what happened that night. I wanted you to know why I did what I did at prom."

Jasmine stiffened. "It was a long time ago."

"I knew what I was doing. I knew your most vulnerable points and I went for the jugular. I've thought of a dozen different things I could have done instead, but back then I was a selfish and naive child. I'm not saying this to make any excuse for myself—God. I'm messing this all up."

"We really don't need to——"

"He was going to drug you," Maddy blurted.

Jasmine's eyes narrowed. "Who?"

"Chris Holt." Bile rose in her throat at the mention of his name. It had been almost a decade since she'd spoken it aloud.

Realization dawned on Jasmine. "So you threw the drink in my face instead of his?"

Maddy cringed. "That's where the dozens of ulterior solutions come in. I heard him tell Brett he was going to . . . well, you caught his eye." She shifted uncomfortably, pushing the memory of those vile words away. Her body tensed, flashes of that night creeping up at the edge of her consciousness. *Just breathe. I can't fall apart here. Josh needs me.* She gripped the edge of the bench and inhaled the sweet, humid air long and deep, grounding herself. "That's why I said what I did about the diseases."

"You were trying to protect me?" Jasmine's voice was incredulous.

Maddy nodded and cast a quick glance at the kids happily playing before she turned back to Jasmine. "I'm sorry I did such a shitty job at it."

Jasmine blinked as if taking it all in. "Why did you hate me so much?"

Maddy leaned against the bench. It was time to face this part. She owed it to Jasmine. "Everyone chose you. My brother, the one who was supposed to be on my side, the only one who knew what it was like at home . . . he chose you and Emma over me. Turner, too."

"What does Turner have to do with any of this?" Jasmine asked.

Maddy sighed. "I really liked him back then. He was the only guy that … I thought he saw me, you know? Through the bullshit act I put on for everyone."

"He is definitely that kind of guy. But Turner and I were only ever friends," Jasmine clarified.

"I know." *But I needed him that night, and I knew he was with you.* It wasn't Jasmine's fault, but back then, it had been easy to blame her too.

"I also recognized that look in your eyes. And I thought, if I could see it in you, you'd discover my secret, too, and then tell everyone just how fake I really was." The confession left her mouth with a whoosh.

Jasmine studied her, tears brimming her gaze. She shifted the baby and patted his back. "Are we talking about . . ."

"My uncle used to keep me overnight when my parents went out for events when I was a child." Maddy's gaze darted to the ground. Apparently today was the day to confess her deepest, darkest secrets.

"When did it stop?" Jasmine's voice cracked.

"When I hit puberty."

Jasmine's hand reached out and rested on Maddy's knee, bringing her a flash of comfort in a dark sea of vile memories.

"I never knew." Jasmine sniffed.

"No one did. I mean, I told my mother once, but . . ."

"Mine didn't help me either." Jasmine's voice had dulled.

Maddy turned towards the kids as they scampered up the slide instead of using the ladder. Zoe's giggle was as infectious as Josh's as they played.

Jasmine let out a deep breath and tugged her shirt down before pulling Hart from the carrier and placing him over her shoulder to burp. "There's a group of us who meet every week who've gone through sexual assault. A therapist oversees it as well as my sister-in-law, Belle—she's a sexual assault nurse examiner. It's been healing for me. If you ever want to go, let me know. Here's my number." Jasmine pulled a business card to The Lighthouse Inn from her pocket and handed it over.

Maddy accepted it, gratefully. "Thank you."

They both turned to their kids on the slide.

After a few moments of weighted silence, Jasmine pointed out, "You left with them on prom night."

Maddy drew her arms across her chest and sat straighter. There was no question who she meant. "Yes." *Worst mistake of my life.*

"And then you disappeared after that."

"Yes."

"There were a lot of rumors going around." Jasmine's voice cracked as she wiped away more tears. She set her son in her lap and handed him a toy before she fixed her watery gaze on Maddy. "I actually almost went out with him after. But Bently wouldn't let me. He said that a few girls had come in throughout the years to the station when he was deputy, and other than hearing his name mentioned and seeing the girls, everything was kept hush-hush from higher up. He wasn't even allowed to look up the files."

There were others? Of course. How could there not be? Should she have said something? Would anyone have believed her?

"You didn't get away, did you?" Jasmine asked, swiping at tears on her face.

Maddy's eyes burned. She pinched her nose and shook her head. Of anyone, Jasmine was the one person who might understand. Instead of seeking friendship, she'd made her an enemy so long ago.

"What's going on here?"

A harsh voice made Maddy jump to her feet.

Turner's eyes focused on Jasmine's tear-filled face as her son squealed in her arms, totally oblivious to the heavy tension between them. His gaze sparked with anger before shifting to disappointment as it landed on Maddy. It was clear he still suspected the worst from her. *He didn't even give me the benefit of the doubt? I guess we haven't made as much progress as I thought.*

"Oh, it's nothing," Jasmine wiped the tears from her eyes.

Turner moved towards Jasmine, running his gaze over her as if seeking an injury before he narrowed his eyes on Maddy, studying her more closely as he asked Jasmine, "Why are you upset?"

He still thinks I'm a monster.

Jasmine looked between Maddy and him before pressing her hand to his chest. "Turner, it's not—"

"No. Forget it. I'll go." Maddy brushed past them.

Jasmine switched her son to one arm and reached for Maddy's elbow. "Maddy—"

Maddy shook her head and whispered only loud enough for Jasmine to hear. "Please don't tell him about what happened."

She continued walking, scooping up a reluctant Josh in her arms.

"But, Mommy, me want to stay. Zoey play!" He squirmed in her arms as she fought the tears.

Turner had disappointed her. He still believed the worst. After she'd shown him her most vulnerable pieces the other day. Once again, she'd been wrong about him. "Maybe next time, bud. We have to go."

"I want TT and Zoey!" He screamed and kicked.

"Please, baby. Just quiet down." He was drawing the stares of an older couple on a bench. *Oh, God.* A woman pushing a stroller gave them a look as they passed down the street, heading back to her car.

She was on the verge of her own breakdown, everything raw and brought to the surface.

"You're a mean mommy!" Josh yelled, and what was left of her self-control snapped. Tears rolled down her face and a sob tore free as she fumbled with the key to unlock her car.

She placed him in his car seat and he fought her the whole way, arching his back like he was possessed.

Maddy gave up and crumpled in the seat next to him, her hands in her face as she cried harder. Joshua quieted.

A moment later, his chubby little hand rested on hers. "I sorry, Mommy."

She pulled him into her arms. "It's not your fault, bud. Mommy's having a hard day."

"Me sing for you. That makes me feel better—when you sing to me." His sweet little voice began the jumbled lyrics to "You are my Sunshine."

She held him a little tighter. "What did I do to deserve such an amazing little boy?"

"You 'mazing, Mommy." He snuggled into her chest.

Inhaling a shaky breath, she settled into the moment, memorizing the curve of his profile and his long eyelashes as they drooped closed. His little hand over her heart, and his even breaths.

"I love you."

You're my reason for everything.

12

TURNER

Turner's heart thumped as Maddy wrangled a squirming Josh down the street. Anxiety churned in his guts. A heavy weight settled in his chest. When he'd come upon the two women, his friend in tears, he'd been thrown back in time. Mixed with his doubts about Maddy, he'd assumed the worst.

"Damn it, Turner." Jasmine sighed.

"Do we have to leave, Mommy?" Zoey asked.

Jasmine shook her head. "No, you can play for a few more minutes."

Zoey ran for the swings.

"What was that all about? Why were you crying?" he asked.

Jasmine swiped at her face, removing the trace of her sorrow. "Because of what we were talking about. She was apologizing to me for high school and prom night."

Prom night? Why did everything come back to that fateful evening?

"What happened that day?"

Jasmine clamped her mouth closed and shook her head, leaning down to press a kiss on her son's temple. "That isn't my story to tell."

Turner sighed and rubbed a hand over the back of his neck.

Jasmine studied him. "Why do you care about what happened to her so much?"

So something did happen. "She's staying at Dad's."

Jaz's eyebrows rose. "Oh."

"I know, it didn't make sense to me either. Apparently he had something to do with that night too."

Jasmine's gaze darted to her daughter as she nodded. "You should give her a chance. The same guys she left with are the same ones who . . ." Jasmine shivered and ran her hands up and down her arms. "Just give her a chance and don't hold her past with me against her."

"Why do you care about her so much suddenly?" He genuinely wanted to know.

Jasmine took a deep breath and let it out before turning to him. Her eyes were glassy once more. "Because Maddy and I have a lot more in common than either of us realized, and none of it is the stuff you want people to know about."

That sinking feeling in his gut became a boulder. *What have I done?*

Turner raced home, breathing a sigh of relief at the sight of her car in the driveway. He pocketed his keys and went inside, then searched the first floor for her. Coming up empty, he took the stairs two at a time. He quietly knocked on her bedroom door and waited.

Soft footsteps padded closer on the other side of the door. The door creaked as she opened it, revealing the darkened room beyond. The sight of her tearstained face sent a spear through his heart.

Her blue eyes hardened as her spine stiffened and her chin jutted out, guarded once more.

"Can we talk?" he whispered.

She peeked over her shoulder at Joshua's tiny body curled on the bed and then stepped out into the hall.

"Uh, do you want to go downstairs, or maybe in here?" He opened his bedroom door.

She didn't look him in the eyes. Instead, she wrapped her arms around herself and walked past him into his room.

His eyes scanned the area. His bed was made, and no stray clothes were left on the floor. Cleanliness was a habit he'd learned in the service.

"Do you want to sit?" He motioned to the bed.

She shook her head.

"Maddy?"

"What?" Her voice was nothing but a whisper. Her hands trembled, and her shoulders rose as if it was taking all her remaining strength to keep the wall between them.

"Why are you really here?"

She breathed out and shook her head. "I told you—"

"Yeah, but why my dad's specifically?"

Her gaze met his. She stared at him for a moment as if trying to read him. "I can see I've overstayed my welcome. I'll go."

He reached out for her, lightly gripping her shoulders. "That isn't what I want. I'm sorry for how I reacted today. I thought—"

"You thought I was bullying Jasmine again . . . and in front of my own child." She shook her head, anger flaming in her eyes quickly clouded by regret. "You must really think I'm a monster."

"No." He exhaled through his nose. "I did think that at first. I'm sorry. I just saw her crying and it pulled me back to . . ."

Her glassy gaze met his. "I really do regret everything I said and did in high school to her and the others. I'd take it all back if I could."

"I know."

"Do you?" She searched his expression.

Did he? Then why did he react that way today? "Why did you leave Shattered Cove after prom and before graduation?"

Her gaze dropped to his chest. "Because I had to."

He stayed silent, hoping she'd say more.

Seconds turned into minutes before she fixed her gaze back on his eyes, her own blurry with tears. Pain wrenched her soul. "She told you, didn't she?"

"Maddy, I—"

A sob tore free as she crumpled to the ground. His arms were quick to slide around her, pulling her onto his lap as he leaned against the bed. Her body shook.

He planted a kiss on her forehead. "She didn't tell me what happened. You don't have to either, but I'm here to listen if you want."

She sniffled. "You want to know why I can't go home?"

Her face tipped towards him. Vulnerability flashed in her blue eyes as her bottom lip trembled, making his heart wrench.

"I told my father what they did to me."

They? Anger lit his veins as he clenched his jaw as tight as he could.

Maddy's voice sounded dull and vacant. "He and my mother didn't answer my calls that night."

Neither did I.

She sucked in a ragged breath and let it out slowly. "He said it was my fault."

Turner's arms tightened around her. He didn't know what happened. But it was clear she'd been hurt—and she'd had to leave town to recover. What the hell had happened to her?

He tightened his grip on her, keeping her safe.

I'm going to kill that motherfucker. All of them.

13

MADDY

The more words tumbled out of Maddy's mouth, the easier it got. She'd never been able to tell anyone these things. Putrid secrets poured from her. Turner's warm embrace gave her the strength she needed. She'd let it all out, and then he'd know just how fucked up she was.

"The first time I told my mother when I was a child that my uncle was . . ." Maddy's throat tightened. Okay, so maybe not every dark secret would be seeing the light of day today. "My mother didn't believe me and told me to stop making up lies."

Turner's grip tightened on her. That small validation gave her the confidence to keep going. "It was like I lived in a doll-house. To the outside, we looked like the perfect family. It got so that I didn't even know who I was anymore. I just played the different parts."

His hand started to rub small circles over her back, bringing her comfort.

"You seemed so happy. I had everyone's attention but the one boy I wanted."

"You liked me?"

She nodded. "And I was so jealous of Jasmine . . . but I also recognized the pain in her eyes, because deep down, we were the same."

Turner's breathing grew shallow. What did he not know about his friend? Would she be betraying that trust?

"I thought she would tell everyone what a fraud I was. My own brother hated me and chose to hang out with her and her friend Emma. So I targeted Jasmine."

"I would have liked you, too, if you weren't . . ."

"A bitch?" She forced a self-deprecating laugh and sat up to look in his eyes.

"Yeah. I thought we had a moment on those bleachers."

She nodded. "We did."

"But then, you threw a drink on Jasmine and said those horrible things." He reminded her.

Her chest tightened. It was now or never. "Chris slipped a roofie into her drink."

Turner's body tensed, his eyes blazing as his jaw pulsed.

"He and Brett were joking about what they would do with a *piece* like that. I hated her, don't get me wrong, but I couldn't let that happen to my worst enemy. So, I got rid of the drink in my usual dramatic fashion and told them she had herpes and possibly HIV so they would leave her alone."

"You saved her."

"In the most mean way possible. I wish I had just gone and told one of the teachers. But I didn't, and that's on me. And trust me, I paid for it." She looked down at her hands. The feel of their hands groping her rushing back to her, as if she were back there in that limo.

"Princess." Turner's thumb grazed her cheek, grounding her back to the moment and forcing her to face him. "Did they hurt you?"

Would he look at her the same after he knew? "Yes."

He tucked her against his chest, holding her tight. Could he not even look at her?

Tears leaked from her eyes.

"I'm so sorry I didn't take your call that night. I should have . . ."

"How could you have known? I was a bitch, and you were doing the honorable thing and taking care of your friend. I won't lie and tell you it didn't hurt, because it did. I thought you saw the real me under the facade, but obviously, I see now how I fucked that up."

Turner's gaze flicked to the door and then back to her. "You called my dad."

She nodded. "He picked me up and brought me home. I told my dad and then . . . he told me it was my fault. I shouldn't have teased them, drank anything, or shown up with them at prom if I didn't expect them to want what was owed. He called my mother to take me away and get me cleaned up. And told me not to say a word about this or everyone would know what a slut I was, and he didn't need anything to ruin his relationship with his business partner, Brett Holt's father."

Turner sucked in a breath, his body trembling against hers. "Christ, he's evil. How the fuck did you survive with parents like that?"

She shook her head. "I ran away. I couldn't take it anymore."

"They told everyone you decided to go traveling abroad before you started college. I thought you were gallivanting across the globe. God, that's so fucked up."

She shrugged and pulled away again, this time sitting beside him with her back against the bed. "That's my life—or it was. Since then, I've been making my own way—trying to, anyways. I had more than a few setbacks in the past few years.

I just needed a safe place to land with my son, and your dad was the only one who was there for me when I needed someone in my life."

Turner ran a hand over his face and released a breath he must have been holding. "And then I came in with my accusations and made it worse."

"I understand why you'd be suspicious."

He turned to her. "Where is Joshua's dad? Is he the mean man Josh was talking about?"

Her eyebrows rose. "No. Kurt was someone I thought I was in love with. Things were perfect, or close to it. Looking back, I can't believe I didn't see the signs. When I got pregnant, the real Kurt made an appearance."

"Did he hurt you?"

"Not in the way you're thinking. I had no idea, but he was a married man."

The blood drained from Turner's face as his eyes widened.

Is he judging me? "I would never have started anything with him had I known. He didn't want anything to do with the baby. He signed away his parental rights in exchange for my silence and not being responsible for child support."

"I'm sorry," Turner said.

"I don't know if this makes me a bad person, but I'm not. I got Joshua from it, and I wouldn't trade him for the world . . . but I won't ever repeat that mistake. I don't ever want to be put in that position again." *And sometimes I wonder if I should reach out to his wife and let her know what a snake she's married to.*

"You're not a bad person." His hand rested over her shoulder, tucking her to his side.

She turned to him. His handsome face so close to hers. He knew everything and he was still here. Still touching her like he cared for her.

Her gaze dropped to his mouth. Would those lips be soft?

Her eyes darted back to his. Want reflected back. The chemistry that had been building for days peaked. And maybe she'd been wrong about him earlier. Hadn't they done enough assuming? She parted her mouth, testing the waters. His focus dropped to the action, his head leaning in just a fraction. *He wants this too.* She wasn't in this alone. She leaned forward and closed her eyes.

Hands dropped to her shoulders and pushed her back. "Maddy."

Her eyes flew open as hot embarrassment crept up her cheeks and neck. She'd misread the situation. She scrambled to her feet. Of course he wouldn't want to touch her after what she'd confessed. She reached for the door handle, but Turner tugged her arm.

"Wait."

She shook her head, pulling away. "I'm sorry—"

Turner gripped her face in his calloused hands, forcing her to look at him. "Stop. You have nothing to be sorry for. I want to kiss you."

What? She stopped pulling away and just stood there.

"You have no idea how bad I want to, but I won't take advantage of you in a vulnerable moment."

Her shoulders drooped as a whoosh left her. What was left of her wall crumbled to the ground to dust. Who was this man? No one ever put her needs first. No one ever cared for her like this.

Warm liquid sunshine spread through her chest, expanding her rib cage. It had been a long time since she'd felt something like that.

Oh, God. I'm falling for Turner.

14

MADDY

Maddy kissed her sleeping son one more time before she snuck out of the room quietly. She walked over to Gerry's bedroom door and knocked softly.

"Come in," he called.

She opened the door and gave him a warm smile.

He looked up from the book he was reading. "Heading to work?"

She nodded.

"See you in the morning." He always sent her off with the sweet reminder that he cared.

"Gerry?"

"Mm-hmm?"

"I know I've said it before, but . . . thank you for everything."

He set his book on the bedside table and slipped his reading glasses off his nose. "You know my wife and I tried for years to have more children but it never happened for us."

Her brows drew together. "I'm sorry."

"We even lost a little girl once, when Turner was about Josh's age."

Maddy placed her hand over her heart, sympathy bleeding from within. "I can't imagine."

He nodded solemnly. "Shortly after that, I was working on your family's estate and caught your father yelling at you for disturbing him in his office for asking him to look at the picture you'd drawn for him."

Maddy's mouth dropped open. *I don't even remember that.* There had been plenty of those times, though, until one day she gave up.

"I was so angry. Why would a man like that be given such a precious gift for him to mistreat when my wife and I wanted another child so badly?"

Gerry thought of her as a precious gift? Maddy fought the tears that blurred her vision.

He sighed and shook his head. "Everything I've done for you, I would do for my own daughter. It's everything you deserve; it's nothing extra special. This is how you should be treated."

"But I'm not your daughter. That's why it means so much to me."

He gave her a smile, his expression softening. "You are now, sweetheart. And that boy is my grandson, no matter what happens. You'll always have a place here." His voice cracked.

Maddy walked farther into the room, wrapped her arms around the older man and gave him a hug. "Thank you."

He cleared his throat as she pulled away, his eyes shining with unshed tears. "Now, you be safe tonight."

She nodded. "I will."

. . .

Maddy made her way outside when a clinking sound came from the garage. She turned, a sliver of light escaping the cracked bay door. She walked up and peered inside. Turner rubbed a red cloth over a tool, cleaning it.

He looked up, a smile curving the corners of his mouth. "Hey."

She pushed the door open more and walked in. His gaze roamed over her done-up face and hair, down to her T-shirt and leggings. The smile faded.

"You heading to the club?" He set the tool on the counter along with the rag.

"Yeah . . . does that bother you?"

He walked up to her, tucking his hands into his pockets. "Don't suppose you'd let me loan you the money you need?"

She shook her head. Maddy had enough for an apartment right now, but she needed a bigger savings for emergencies, and working part-time in landscaping wasn't going to cut it. The money from the club was just too good to pass up.

He sighed. "It's your body, and if dancing at the club makes you happy, then it's none of my business."

It didn't make her happy. Exotic dancing had never been her dream. Not like some of the girls who loved their work at The Pearl Necklace. And of all the clubs she'd worked at, that was the best. The rules were strict and enforced. The women wore collars specific to what their boundaries were. Prostitution was illegal, and Maddy had never even considered it. She was strictly a dancer. But the red room in the back was for those *other* activities and the people who were willing to pay for less-than-legal services. Maddy didn't know how it all worked beyond the curtain, and she didn't want to. The owner was a scary man, but he was fair. And the mayor was a frequent visitor—along with the chief of police—to the red room. That was probably why it was allowed to continue. That or the fact that, as rumor had it, the club owner was related to the Carelli family.

"Maddy?" Turner asked, bringing her back to the moment.

"It's just work. It pays the bills. It's not what I want forever . . ." She looked away, embarrassed. "You promise you don't think less of me for it?"

He stepped closer, his knuckles skimming her cheek. She shivered. The scent of engine oil mixed with his natural spicy scent.

Turner's Caribbean-blue eyes locked on hers, intense and hungry. He dipped his head, melding his lips with hers. Fireworks exploded in her belly, bursting as hot arousal pooled in her center. His sweet tongue traced the seam of her lips. She opened for him, sucking on it. He groaned, tightening his hands on her waist before nipping her bottom lip and then deepening the kiss. His touch burned her with yearning. She clutched his shirt, holding on for dear life as he gave her the kiss of a lifetime. Spinning her up until she was on top of the world.

He pulled away, tipping his forehead to hers. "As long as you come home to me, princess."

15

MADDY

A heady, sexy beat pulsed through the club as Maddy made her rounds. Dolly, one of the other strippers, threw her head back and laughed at something the suit across from her said. Her eyes caught Maddy's and she waved her over. Maddy adjusted her breasts in the black mesh crop top and headed towards Dolly.

Her friend had her blond hair tied into pigtails. Dolly's costume was that of the typical naughty Catholic schoolgirl with the plaid micro miniskirt and tied white button-up, of which none of the snaps were actually done. Maddy giggled to herself at the irony of the costume. Dolly's act was a naive young woman, and she played the role well despite having her master's in biology. She worked to pay for her PHD, and was set to graduate in the spring debt-free thanks to this club.

"My friend Scarlett might be interested." Dolly stood, revealing the man across from her.

Maddy's smile dropped. Her stomach turned to solid stone as she froze. Her body went rigid and ice cold as the blood drained from her face. Her heart thudded so loud it drowned out the thumping music in the club.

Chris Holt sat on the blue velvet cushions, arms and legs wide just like he owned the place. Just like he had in the limo.

Dolly wrapped an arm around her, pulling her partly from her panic. Her friend cut her a curious glance. "Chris here wants to see a little girl-on-girl action. You want to dance with me?" She leaned closer to Maddy's ear and whispered, "He offered five thousand for the night. Maybe that's worth you ditching the black collar just this once?"

Maddy opened her mouth but nothing came out. Her skin itched, everything in her screaming at her to run. But she couldn't leave her friend with this monster.

"You're shaking." Dolly spoke through her fake smile and gave Chris a wink.

Maddy risked a glance at Chris. Bile rose in her throat. A satisfied smirk crossed his face as his cold empty gaze raked over her. Violation churned inside her, soaking her in vulnerability.

Tears burned her eyes as he watched her like a cat ready to play with his prey. No, she wouldn't be a victim again. She wasn't a young girl trapped like she had been. Here, in this club, she held some power.

"Dolly, tell Buddy there's a gold member at table six. We want to make sure our customer only gets the very best experience."

Her friend stiffened at the coded reference. The owner had a collection of phrases set up to protect his workers. That was one of the reasons she chose this club after the disaster of her last job.

"He likes the double-girl action. Why don't you come with me?" She tugged Maddy's arm. There was supposed to be safety in numbers, after all. Maddy's chest tightened. She wasn't alone this time.

Chris stood, his dark eyes alert. Maddy stepped back instinctively as he approached her.

"Hey, sweetie, we'll get your room all set and then we'll come get you." Dolly stepped in front of Maddy, placing her hand on Chris's arm. Her friend's protective gesture would not be forgotten.

Chris shook his head and sneered, gripping her wrist. "Don't fucking touch me, bitch."

Dolly's smile evaporated. "Let me go, asshole."

Chris ignored her and turned his attention to Maddy. "Been a long time, Madeline."

"Not long enough," she gritted out. Her body trembled, her heart racing, her stomach twisting itself into knots. *Where are the bouncers?* Dolly's eyes searched the room as if asking the same question.

"You remember what happened last time you got between me and a good time." Chris leaned closer, releasing Dolly's hand. Her friend grabbed Maddy's arm and tugged her away but Chris grabbed the back of her neck, pulling her against him.

Her skin crawled as she heaved and pushed him away, but he didn't budge. Panic tore through her. She was trapped again. *Oh, God. Trapped, and there's nothing I can do. No. Not again.*

"Sometimes I still watch the video of that night. Of you begging us to stop."

She froze, chills piercing her skin like tiny daggers. Terror clawed her insides to ribbons. *There was a video?*

"I'll tell everyone what a monster you are." Her voice came out strangled as she lifted her knee as hard as she could.

He bowed over and yelped in pain. His angry face snarled

at her as Buddy finally appeared, taking hold of the man who had stolen a piece of her she'd never get back.

Chris laughed as he stood, struggling against the bouncer. "Who's gonna believe a stripper over me?"

Buddy pushed him towards the exit as they garnered a room full of stares.

"This isn't over!" Chris called, as the heads of several patrons turned to stare. After Chris disappeared out the door, a few people turned their heads to her, their expressions curious.

"Why is a woman's word worth so much less than a man's? How many women's voices would it take to equal one man's?" Maddy asked the question aloud.

Dolly wrapped her arm around her as their friend Candy did the same from the other side. They may have not known each other's real names, but they were true friends who looked out for one another in the club.

"You okay?" Candy asked.

Maddy nodded numbly. She needed to wash the feel of that man off her. She'd sworn he would never touch her again and he'd managed to do just that. *But this time I fought back.*

"You need a drink." Candy tugged her towards the bar, getting Veronica's attention behind the counter. "Give the girl something strong."

Veronica nodded, setting a glass on the bar top in front of them and pouring a clear liquid into it before pushing it towards Maddy.

Maddy accepted it, taking the shot and slamming it down as she squinted, relishing the burn. "Another." She didn't normally drink, but to finish her shift, she'd need something to help her through. Her gaze searched the crowd, looking for something to help divert her attention. She needed to escape this feeling.

"Here you go." Veronica topped off the glass. Maddy took the second shot. The burn wasn't as bad that time. She breathed out and nodded.

"You want to chill in the back room for a while?" Dolly asked.

Maddy shook her head. No. She needed to do what she came here for and make money. And, most of all, she needed to escape.

"I need to dance." She weaved through the tables full of men drinking and chatting with other dancers, or in rapt attention of the routine being performed on the left side of the stage. She walked towards one of the empty poles on the right side of the room. Gripping the brass pole, she spun round it, closing her eyes and moving her body to the beat. Alcohol rushed through her veins, relaxing her, adding a fuzzy tint to the room. Dolly's hand gripped the pole above her, her friend grinding against her. This wasn't the first time they'd done this. It always attracted attention. And here, attention meant money.

"You good?" Dolly asked, her hand sliding around Maddy's waist.

"I will be." Maddy twisted, gripping the back of Dolly's neck, ready to play her part in their routine. Dressed in all black, eyes dark with kohl, lips bloodred, Maddy slipped into her role of Scarlett the harlot. Dolly dropped to her knees, selling her innocent act, her hands running up and down Maddy's thighs. Maddy whined her hips seductively before she turned to Dolly, running her nose over the woman's shoulder, up her neck, inhaling her sweet perfume.

Catcalls and suggestive comments were shouted all around them as hungry gazes watched on. Money rained down on the stage. A few hands reached out, tucking bills into her thigh-highs. Maddy untied Dolly's top, setting her breasts free. Dolly shimmied and danced on the stage before getting on all fours. Maddy lifted up the back of her skirt before tearing it off at the snaps. The men around them cheered and shouted their approval. Maddy risked a glance. Hungry, glazed, lustful eyes were all aimed at her and her friend. The women held the real power here. Maddy lapped the control up.

"I think Dolly's been a very bad girl," she shouted to the crowd.

"Yeah!"

"Punish her!"

Maddy leaned down and spoke to Dolly, seeking her permission for this next part. "You ready for your spanking?"

Dolly bit her lip and fluttered her eyelashes. "I don't know."

Maddy smiled. This was all part of the plan. "You hear that, gentlemen? Dolly here might need some more convincing."

Dollars hit the stage.

"Oh, come on, you can do better than that," Maddy cried. "Help me teach Dolly how to be a good girl."

Bigger bills fell to the stage. Maddy smiled. She ran her hands over Dolly's ass. "Ready for your punishment?"

"Yes!" Dolly's voice turned pleading. The woman knew how to work a crowd.

Maddy pulled her hand back and struck her once, twice. Dolly played her part, moaning and whimpering, promising to be an obedient little slut. The crowd ate it up, money raining onto the stage.

Once it was over, Maddy helped Dolly to her feet before her friend asked, "Who wants to get a drink with me?"

Maddy surveyed the crowd and froze.

Blue eyes engulfed in flames of lust locked on hers. *Turner.* Would he be disgusted by her performance?

Maddy handed Dolly the clothing she'd torn off her before walking off the stage into the crowd of men, heading towards Turner.

"How much for the two of you in the red room for a private show?" one man asked as she tried to pass.

"Maddy isn't a red collar, so she stays out here. But I can find another friend to have some fun with back there if you want?" Dolly answered for her.

Maddy made her way to the edge of the crowd. Turner leaned against the wall, arms across his chest. The red lights illuminated his sexy features. Only a slight buzz remained from the alcohol. The energy thrumming through her veins was adrenaline from her show. Why was he here?

As long as you come home to me, princess.

Was he really okay with this? Did it matter? What was she to him? That goodbye earlier said he wanted more. And one look at him and some of the tension she'd carried from her encounter with Chris eased. But it was still there, in the sharp edges of her consciousness.

"Hey."

"Can we get a room?" he asked, his gaze darkened, raking over her.

She nodded and led him to the rooms for private lap dances. He pulled out his credit card and handed it over to the bouncer at the door.

"Blue room." Lenny nodded them through.

Maddy opened the door. His heat rushed her back as the door shut behind them. The music changed to something slow and smooth with a seductive beat. His hands rested on her upper arms, burning her skin with his gentle touch. He spun her around, their gazes locked before his mouth crashed to hers.

16

MADDY

Turner's mouth was heaven and hell. Maddy sucked in a gasp as his teeth raked over her bottom lip. His hands threaded through her hair, and he pulled her closer to him like he couldn't get enough. She wasn't wearing much, but it felt like too much as their passion consumed her.

A low growl rumbled in his chest as he ground his hard cock against her. "You're so fucking sexy. I can't think straight when I'm around you."

She hooked her arms over his neck, kissing him, tasting him with her tongue. His large hands dropped to her ass, picking her up. She wrapped her legs around him. He carried her over to the chair in the center of the room and sat down.

She ground against him as he devoured her mouth, his hands moving to explore and touch her body. He squeezed her breasts and she let out a whimper.

"What do you need, princess?"

"This." She kissed him harder.

His fingers dug into her thighs before he slipped a hand

beneath the strap of leather and pushed her thong aside, dipping two fingers inside her.

She gasped.

"You're so goddamned wet. Is this for me?"

She nodded, her eyes hazy. She was intoxicated with overwhelming need.

He pumped those fingers in and out of her, curling them until the tips pressed against the sweet spot inside her. She bit her lip, trying to stay quiet. These rooms were not for sex, and if Lenny heard them, he'd bust in here. The boss was strict on his rules. Sex only happened in the red room.

Turner slipped his fingers from her pussy. She clenched her inner walls at the loss, whimpering.

He opened his mouth. His eyes locked with hers as he slid his fingers between his lips. He licked them clean. The heat in his gaze made her squirm on his lap. "You taste fucking delicious."

Her breaths came in pants, her core aching for him. She reached for the button on his pants, undoing it.

Turner lifted his hips enough for her to shimmy them off him. His cock jutted out, engorged and already leaking precum. She licked her lips, wanting to taste him too. He reached to the back pocket of the pants on the floor, grabbed a foil packet from his wallet. He held it out to her. She took it and ripped it open before sliding the latex over his cock wordlessly.

The blue lights in the room cast him in monochromatic beauty as she lowered herself over him. He hissed and gripped her hips, holding her steady, forcing her to take this slow. His eyes locked on hers as her pussy hungrily took every inch of him. She wrapped her hands around his neck, kissing him as she started to ride. He grunted, his hands gripping her tighter as she fucked him closer and closer to his orgasm.

"Play with your nipples," he ordered, his hands digging

into her hips as he controlled her pace. She squeezed her hard buds through the mesh shirt, a zinging sensation of arousal spiraling through her.

"God, you're so sexy." His praise only fueled her on. She arched her back, thrusting her chest closer to his face. He leaned forward, capturing one of her nipples into his mouth as his other hand found her clit.

"Oh!" She bit her lip again, stifling her cry.

"That's it, princess. Come all over me." He swirled his thumb, bringing her to the brink of pleasure. His cock pulsed inside her as his muscles grew taut. Teeth nicked her sensitive nipples, sending her over the edge. She tensed over him, his name coming from her mouth in a strangled whisper.

"Maddy," he groaned, his arms locking around her as he drove his hips into her a final time. His dick jerked.

Her chest heaved as the song ended, fading out before another started.

He leaned back, a dopey smile on his face. "That was . . ."

"Yeah." She smiled, not ready to get off him or for this moment to be over.

"How much for the night?" he asked.

Maddy froze, her smile dropping like the stone in the pit of her stomach. Her gaze roamed around the room over his discarded pants. This was just sex to him. *And he paid me for it.* He thought she was a prostitute. *And I just broke my one rule.* Because this wasn't business for her. She'd thought they'd had a connection. Apparently she'd been wrong. He'd used her.

She got up, stumbling for the doorknob.

"Maddy, wait!"

Her nerves were still raw from her encounter with Chris from earlier, and now this. Turner was the one man she'd thought maybe could be different. Hadn't they made progress? Hadn't he made it clear he wanted something more with her?

And then he went and asked to pay me for the night.

"I'm not a whore," she growled before running out the door and slamming it behind her. There was nothing wrong with having sex for money, but she had never done so. That line of sex work wasn't for her. That was her hard limit in this industry. *Until two minutes ago.*

Lenny's questioning glance met hers.

She forced a tight smile. "That guy will need a minute."

Lenny nodded and folded his hands back across his belly. It wasn't uncommon that some of their customers needed some time alone after a session, and they'd always pay extra for it.

Maddy made her way to the back lounge for the dancers, to the bathroom, locking herself in an empty stall. A sob broke through her resolve once she was alone. "How could I think a man would actually want me for me and not my body?"

It seemed even the man she'd always held on a pedestal couldn't live up to the most basic expectation. To him she was an object—just like she was to all the rest of them.

She hugged her arms closer and lowered her head. "Fuck him. Fuck them all."

She was done being used.

17

TURNER

Turner's leg bounced as he waited in the living room for Maddy's return. Headlights lit the driveway as her car pulled in. He stood, pacing in the dim room as the motion-sensor lights flicked on outside. He ran a hand nervously through his hair as Maddy exited the car, shoulders slumped. Her hair had been pulled back in a ponytail, and the dark mascara trailed down her cheeks. She swiped her hand across her eyes and his chest constricted. She was crying and it was his fault. The sight of her in pain sent daggers through his heart.

She turned towards the window, her face falling as she stopped. Her chest heaved as if she were taking a deep breath before her spine straightened, and she continued to the front door.

Turner walked to the entrance and opened the door for her. She walked in, keeping her chin held high as she brushed past him.

"Maddy, I'm sorry. I didn't mean how that came out."

She kept walking. "Save it."

Turner reached out, gripping her arm to stop her.

Maddy yanked her arm away, her eyes glistening with a mixture of tears and fear. A rock sank in his stomach. He was the cause of both.

"Princess, please—"

"Don't call me that," she hissed. She reached into her bag and threw a wad of cash at him, money raining on the floor. "Regardless of what you think, I'm not a prostitute. Keep your damn cash." She spun around and ran up the stairs.

He let out a defeated sigh.

"Fuck," he swore under his breath and clenched his fists. He needed to fix this.

He walked up the stairs as the water in the bathroom turned on. Turner leaned his forehead against the door. She needed a night's rest. He'd talk to her tomorrow and fix this.

After a fitful few hours of tossing and trying to sleep, Turner gave up and headed down to make coffee. His dad wished him a good day and then took off to golf. Turner pulled out all the fixings for waffles and got to work. A little while later, a small figure entered the kitchen.

Josh rubbed his eyes, some sort of action figure in one of his hands. "Are you making breakfast?"

Turner smiled. "Yup. But I could use a helper for the chocolate chips."

Josh's eyes rounded. "You put chocolate in breakfast?"

"Sometimes. Come on up here and pour them in for me." Turner pulled a chair across to the counter.

Josh set his toy on the table and climbed up. Turner handed him a measuring cup with the last ingredient. The boy eagerly swiped a few for his mouth and spun away as if Turner wouldn't know what he'd been up to.

Turner chuckled. "Save some for the waffles, bud."

A guilty-looking Josh turned back to him, eyes alert as if studying Turner's reaction.

"Pour them in."

Josh lifted the steel cup and dumped the contents into the batter, a few mini chips escaping onto the counter.

"Now stir it up." Turner kept an eye on the little man as he swirled the batter, giggling. "That's it. Perfect."

"What are you doing?" Maddy's shaky voice cut through the reverie.

Turner spun around. Maddy's eyes were puffy and red and rimmed in dark shadows as if she had cried all night and barely slept.

"Me make breakfast, Mommy!" Josh announced proudly. He thrust the whisk up—but the edge of the instrument caught on the bowl, sending it flying on the ground before Turner could catch it.

"Shit." Turner stared at the mess on the floor.

"Shit," Josh parroted.

Turner winced and looked up to Maddy.

She closed her eyes as if counting to ten.

"I sorry, TT." Josh set the whisk down on the counter.

"It's okay, bud. Accidents happen. Just means we'll have to go to the diner for breakfast."

"Yay!" Josh cheered and clapped his hands, wobbling on the chair.

"Careful, bud." Turner reached out to steady him but Maddy beat him to it.

She picked up her son, tucking him away from Turner. "Josh, go upstairs and get dressed. I laid out your clothes on the bed."

"Otay. Can I get chocolate panny-cakes at the diner?" he asked.

"We're staying here for breakfast," she corrected him.

"There's nothing here; I used the last of the eggs. Besides, I know the owners and they make exceptions for little boys who listen to their mamas. They might just add a few chocolate chips to your pancakes if you ask real polite," Turner interjected. He wasn't going to let her avoid talking to him, and he was going to show her last night had been one big misunderstanding. They wouldn't be able to talk in front of Josh, but the least he could do was get her and her kid a proper breakfast first.

"Yay!" Josh scampered up the stairs.

Maddy turned on him, her eyes blazing. "What the hell do you think you're doing?"

He stepped around the batter mess. "We need to talk."

"I have nothing to say to you."

"Well, then you can listen. Because I have a lot to tell you."

"Mommy!"

She shook her head and disappeared up the stairs.

This wouldn't be easy, but then again nothing ever truly worth it was.

Turner opened the door to the diner and Maddy and Josh filtered in. Maddy hadn't said a single word to him since the fiasco in the kitchen. Josh seemed to be happy to fill the silence, chatting about some cartoon characters he loved.

Maddy chose a booth in the corner and slid in next to Josh. Turner took the opposite side.

"Welcome back." Brynn handed them menus and took out a coloring page and packet of crayons for Josh.

"Can I have chocolate chip panny-cakes, pease?" Josh asked.

Brynn's gaze softened as she looked at the little boy. "If your parents say it's okay."

Maddy's eyes widened, her attention snapping to Turner's and then Brynn's. "Oh, he's not—we're not together."

Like hell they weren't. But he was already skating on thin ice. He wasn't going to chance a teasing comeback. It was his mouth that had gotten him into this predicament in the first place.

"So sorry," Brynn apologized.

"Nothing to be sorry for. I'll take the breakfast deluxe, an order of chocolate chip pancakes for Josh, with orange juice, and what do you want, Maddy?" Turner handed the menu back to Brynn.

"Just some yogurt with fruit, please."

"Be right up. Coffee, anyone?"

"Yes, please." Maddy offered the woman a small smile.

"Me too, thank you," Turner added.

Brynn nodded and took off.

"Look, Mommy, it's a shark this time." Josh held up his coloring page.

"So cool." Maddy focused on her son, the stress draining from the tense lines in her forehead until they disappeared.

"Maddy?" a deep voice asked next to their table.

Turner faced the man, recognizing him immediately. George Miller, Maddy's brother.

"Geo?" Maddy's voice trembled as she got to her feet.

"It is you. Jasmine told me you were here. Where have you been?" Geo asked, pulling her into a hug.

Maddy's shoulders relaxed as she hugged her brother back. She pulled away, her eyes watery with tears. "Here and there."

"Mommy?" Josh asked, grabbing her hand.

"You have a kid?" Geo asked. His jaw dropped open.

Maddy gave him a sheepish smile. "Josh, this is your uncle Geo."

"You have a lot of tattoos," Josh pointed out.

Geo chuckled and bent down to Josh's level. "Comes with the job of being a rock star."

Josh's eyes grew wide. "You're a rock star?"

"Sure am. You play anything?"

Josh shook his head. "I'm only free." He held up three fingers.

"We'll have to change that. Get you a guitar like your uncle."

"Can I, Mommy?" Josh asked, jumping up and down in his seat excitedly.

"We'll see," Maddy answered.

Geo stood and cut a glance at Turner. "Hey, man. I had no idea you two were together."

"We're not," Maddy corrected before he could say anything. "I'm staying at Turner's dad's house for a little while."

Geo's eyes flickered between the two of them. His eyebrow rose.

"Not yet," Turner added.

Maddy shot him a glare.

"You seen Mom and Dad yet?" Geo asked.

Vulnerability flashed in Maddy's gaze, and Turner wanted to wrap his arms around her and tell her it would all be okay. But that would only make things worse. Did Geo not know how they'd treated her?

"No."

Geo nodded as if he understood. "I'm only in town for a little while before I head on tour. We should catch up. What's your number?" Geo pulled out his phone.

Maddy took it and input her contact info.

"I missed you, Maddy." Geo pulled her into a hug. "Don't you fucking disappear again without telling me."

"I didn't think you cared," Maddy confessed, defensively.

Geo pulled away enough to look at her. "Don't lump me in with them. I know we never got along, but you're my twin sister. I care."

Her throat bobbed as her eyes welled with tears. She nodded.

"Enjoy your breakfast. Nice meeting you, Josh. Turner." Geo nodded towards him.

Turner waved goodbye as Maddy took her seat once more, a small smile playing on her lips. Her eyes shone brighter than they had been when they'd walked in here.

Her gaze flicked to his. The light blinked out. Regret sloshed in his stomach.

Brynn set their coffee and drinks on the table. Maddy thanked her, but Turner's guts had already turned to acid.

Maddy truly had no one—not even her own twin brother had been by her side during the last eight years. And Turner had made a complete fool of himself and been an asshole to her.

He'd made her feel cheap last night. How could he convince her she was quickly becoming one of the most precious things in his life? Or were they too far gone?

No. He wouldn't believe it. He'd make this right, somehow. Starting the moment he got her alone.

18

MADDY

Maddy's heart ached at the sight of her son, sleeping soundly against Turner's shoulder. When Brynn had mistaken them for a family, Maddy had wished for one second that it was true. But then reality came crashing back. Turner might have a sweet side to him when it came to Josh, but he'd used her just like every man who came before. With any other man, she'd think his kindness towards her son was an act, but she knew him enough to have confidence it wasn't.

She opened the door for him and followed him up to the room she shared with Josh. Turner laid him on the bed before taking off his shoes and covering him up. Turner ran his hand over Josh's forehead before standing. His gaze locked on hers. She crossed her arms across her chest and looked away.

Turner picked her up, throwing her over his shoulder. She gasped. Bastard knew she couldn't yell and wake her child. He carried her across the hall to his room and shut the door with his foot before putting her down.

Maddy pushed him away, a tingle of fear trickling down her spine. Would Turner hurt her? Would he . . .

Turner must have seen it because he held his hands up and backed up to the door. "I just need to talk to you . . . please?"

"I think you said enough last night." She crossed her arms again, an attempt to shield herself from the emotions running rampant in her chest.

"After you left, I was worried about you, so I went to the club. I hated that all those other men got to look at you. I know I have no right, but it bothered me because you told me this wasn't something you would have chosen if you had other options. It would be different if this was actually something you wanted."

"You got jealous, and thought you'd what? Prove a point?"

He shook his head. "No. I wanted to help you. You won't take a loan, so I thought a lap dance was the way to go. I planned to pay for your whole night, be your only, uh, customer. I never expected to have sex with you."

Maddy swallowed, her eyes flitting wildly around the room as she tried to digest what he'd said. Could she trust him? Had he really been just trying to help her and save her pride?

"Why?"

"Why do I want to help?" Turner asked.

"Yes, and why did it go further last night?" For her, she'd wanted to replace Chris's hands; she'd wanted to take back that power. And her self-control had finally broken because of the sexual chemistry between them. Those light blue eyes of his had *seen* her. Or so she'd thought.

Turner took a deep breath and released it as his gaze locked with hers. "Because I have feelings for you."

"What kind of feelings?" she probed. There was no room in her life for hoping for the impossible.

He stepped forward, his hand rising to brush his knuckles over her cheek. "The kind that only get stronger with time. The kind that make me want things with you that I have no business wanting."

"What are you saying?"

He stepped even closer, leaning in, his breath tickling her lips. "I'm saying I'm not going anywhere. I'm gonna earn your trust and make up for being an asshole. And I hope you'll forgive me, princess, because I've never regretted anything as much as causing you pain." He tipped his forehead to hers.

She closed her eyes. The sexual tension in the room thick enough to cut with a knife. Could she trust him? Everything in her screamed to give in. Her wounded heart raced against her chest.

"When you hurt, I feel it here." He picked up her hand and spread it over his heart, enveloping her small hand with his.

Something broke in her chest, a dam of some sort—and liquid warmth poured through the cracks and splinters filling her rib cage. She opened her eyes and pulled back enough to search his for any sign of dishonesty.

"Maddy." Her name bled from his lips like a plea.

The energy in the room shifted. She was standing on the precipice—the edge of a cliff. If she gave in to this, she'd be free-falling into the unknown. Would he be there to catch her in his solid arms? There was only one way to find out.

She closed her eyes and crashed her mouth against his. Turner didn't respond at first, as if in shock, and then his arms tightened around her. His hands splayed over her back between her shoulder blades and down to her waist.

She slipped her tongue in his mouth, cinnamon dancing on her taste buds. He groaned, pressing his body closer to her. She stumbled back, looping her arms around his neck, taking him with her as she fell onto the bed. His weight settled over her as the bed springs creaked and groaned.

He pulled back, eyes hazy and surprised. "I want more than this. We don't have to do anything sexual. I just want to be with you."

And that, right there, sealed the deal for her. Each truth tearing down what was left of her barriers. "And that's why I want this," she whispered against his lips before capturing his mouth once more with hers.

His hands slipped up her thighs as he thrust his hard cock between them, too many clothes separating them. Turner pulled away a second time. "Are you sure? I don't want to fuck this up again."

Maddy let a groan of protest escape before she reached down and cupped his dick. "I'm sure. I want you."

"Fuuuuck." He clenched his jaw as if fighting with his last thread of control. "Okay, but this is about you."

His lips slipped between hers again. Their kiss turned feverish. Her fingers raked through his hair, tugging as he deepened the kiss, his hands roaming over her breasts. He slipped his warm calloused palms under her T-shirt, cupping her breasts.

A quiet moan left her lips.

"Ssshhh. Be quiet, princess, or I'll give you something to fill that pretty mouth of yours," Turner whispered.

Heat pooled in her sex, leaking from her pussy at his dark promise. Turner nuzzled her neck, inhaling as he kissed a trail between her breasts, down her belly. Hooking his fingers under the elastic of her shorts, he tugged them down her legs until her bottom half was exposed.

Big hands pressed her thighs apart, baring her pussy to him. "God, you're so beautiful."

She shivered. Her eyes locked on him. His gaze hungrily locked on her sex.

He licked his lips and flicked his attention to her. "Don't make a sound, or I'll have to stop. You understand, sweetheart?"

She nodded. How long had it been since a man had gone down on her? The last relationship she'd had was with Josh's father, and he almost never had. Sex with him had been more about his pleasure. But even last night at the club, Turner had made sure to get her off before he came himself.

His head slipped between her legs, the scruff of his beard rubbing against the sensitive flesh. She shivered in anticipation.

"Watch me make you come," Turner ordered.

Maddy sat up on her elbows as he spread her pussy lips with his fingers. Her body trembled under his reverent touch. Turner leaned in, his tongue darting out and licking up her slit. She sucked in a sharp breath, her chest rising and falling more rapidly as he continued his ministrations.

"Mmmmm, so fucking good." Turner hummed and lapped up her juices, one hand massaging her pussy while that wicked muscle lapped at her clit, winding her closer and closer to her orgasm. Pressure built, swirling and spinning inside her.

Turner slipped two fingers into her tight hole, curling them to hit her G-spot. Her eyes widened, her gaze sharpening as she arched her back off the bed. Whimpers and pleas escaped her mouth.

"Shhhh. I'll get you there, princess. Lie back and let me worship this cunt. Not gonna stop until you come all over my face. Want the evidence painted on me. Trust me to take care of you, baby."

Through hazy, wanton vision, Maddy managed a nod as

she relaxed into the bed. The rising pleasure winding through her body captured her attention. Turner sucked on her clit and then switched his rhythm, gently licking all around it. Her muscles tensed. She writhed, frantic and needy as he massaged her mound, smoothing her juices around her swollen flesh. His fingers thrust in and out of her, fucking her with a steady rhythm, hitting her G-spot each time they entered her. He lowered his mouth to her clit once more, sucking and humming at the same time. Her orgasm crashed through her, the pressure in her core releasing with a gush of liquid squirting down her legs. She bit down on her lip, caging her screams. Every muscle tensed as a tsunami of ecstasy crashed over and swallowed her up until she was left floating in warm euphoria.

Turner licked her thighs, his fingers still slowly fucking her as she came down. He climbed next to her, his beard shiny with her arousal. A satisfied smirk twisted up his mouth.

His awe-filled eyes searched her face. "You okay?"

"I'll let you know when I return to my body."

He chuckled. "You squirted all over me."

Embarrassment heated her cheeks. "Oh God, I'm sorry."

His brows drew together before he lowered his mouth to hers, sharing her essence in the most intimate of kisses. "It was the sexiest thing I've ever seen."

"Seriously?"

His eyes glittered with lust. "I'm just wondering how many times I can make you do that before Josh wakes up."

She giggled. "What about you? It's your turn next."

He shook his head. "No, this is about you."

"But—"

"Shhh. Making you come is pleasure enough for me. You make me feel like a fucking god."

Was this man for real? "You don't want to come?"

"In time. Right now, I want to explore every inch of your body and learn how to drive you crazy."

She blinked and looked at his chest.

Turner's finger tipped her chin, forcing her to look in his eyes. "Don't hide from me. I'm not like them."

Was he reading her mind now?

"Don't bring anyone else into this bed but me. I don't share, even up here." He tapped her temple. "Give us a chance. I promise I'll do everything in my power to prove to you I'm not going anywhere."

"Ever?" she teased, trying to make light of the seriousness that had descended upon them.

Turner locked eyes with her. "Not if I have anything to say about it."

Her mouth dropped open. How could he mean that? It wasn't like he was falling in love with her . . . was he?

19

MADDY

Maddy wiped the sweat from her brow and relaxed into the seat as the air conditioner blasted over her.

"Here." Turner handed her a cold bottle of water.

She unscrewed the cap and drank the icy liquid down, cooling her core. He did the same.

He set the bottle down and shifted the car into gear. "I've got one more yard to do, but I'll drop you off home first."

Home. Butterflies tumbled in her belly. Gerry Walker's house had been the only place that had ever felt like home. And now that things had changed between her and Turner, it was like she could finally let go of that breath she'd been holding while bracing herself for everything to fall apart.

"No, I'll help you. We'll get it done faster together." She took a sip of the water bottle in the console.

He peeked over at her as he pulled them onto the main road. "I think maybe you should sit this one out."

Her brows drew together as she twisted in her seat to face him. "Why?"

He cleared his throat. "Our next client is your parents."

Her chest cinched tight as if a boa constrictor wound around it, squeezing out all the air in her lungs. Her stomach hardened and her skin prickled. Was she ready to go back there? She hadn't even driven by yet. What if she ran into one of them?

"I'll take you home." Turner's hand stretched out, landing on her thigh and giving her a light squeeze. He'd done a one-eighty from when she'd first gotten here, going from hating her to trying to protect her. She exhaled, some of the tension leaving her shoulders. Turner would be there. She wouldn't be alone this time. Her parents were unlikely to even come out. They hardly ever mingled with lower-class people if they didn't have to, unless it was for a photo op at a charity function.

She lifted her chin and set her shoulders. "No. I'll go."

"You sure?" His head swiveled towards her, concern marring his sweat-slicked forehead.

She nodded, her chin tipping up defiantly. She wouldn't let her parents have this control over her anymore. "I'm sure."

The rest of the ride was quiet. Her nerves twisted her stomach, making her nauseous. Turner flipped on the radio. Country music filtered in from the speaker as he guided the truck towards the wealthier side of Shattered Cove. With each street, the houses got bigger and more spaced out. Maddy's heart thumped against her rib cage as her parents' grand chateau-style home came into view.

Memories of her childhood skittered over her. Her hands grew clammy as Turner slipped the car into park.

"You sure you're up for this?"

She nodded. "Let's get to work."

She opened the door and climbed back into the heat. There was a BMW in the driveway. Her parents' vehicles were always stored in the garage, so it was impossible to tell if they were home or not. But someone was.

"Let's get the trees unloaded first, and then I'll get the mower off the trailer. You want to do that or the trim?"

"The trim." She slipped on the heavy-duty gloves and climbed onto the back of the truck to grab one of the trees.

After unloading, she grabbed the weed wacker and got to work, casting glances towards the house. *Is Mom or Dad in there? Can they see me out here? Would they know it was me?*

She finished up the back, risking a peek into the window to her father's office. Empty. The steady thrum of the lawn mower droned in the background as Turner passed over the yard. Maddy adjusted her sunglasses and continued her work around the side of the house. After finishing, she loaded the tool back into the truck.

A few weeds from the flower bed in front caught her eye. Maddy walked over and bent to pull them up as the front door opened and her mother strolled out with another woman she didn't recognize. Maddy straightened her spine, a habit from all those years spent under a microscope and ingrained during the classes on etiquette. A part of her wished she could hide in the background and another hoped her mother would finally see her and . . .and what? It wasn't like she expected a family reunion. Her mother had never been the maternal, loving type. Since having Josh, Maddy's resentment for her parents had grown. How could a mother treat a child the way hers had? For that matter, how could a father? Was she simply unlovable? She'd done everything they'd wanted and it had gotten her nowhere. She'd always fallen short.

Her mother, Susan, laughed at something her guest said as they both turned towards her. Her mother's smile dropped, her gaze quickly roaming over Maddy. Suddenly self-conscious, Maddy tucked a strand of hair behind her ear. Her mother quickly shook her head and smiled even brighter at her friend before turning her back on Maddy and walking towards the BMW.

Maddy stood there, frozen. *What did I really expect?*

A strong arm slipped around her shoulders. She turned as Turner's sweat-streaked face, shaded by a ball cap, came into her vision. Why was he blurry?

His thumb wiped under her eyes as hot tears trickled down her cheeks. *Oh, that's why.* Hadn't she wasted enough tears on her mother? Why was it so hard to kill the ember of hope inside?

Turner tipped her chin up with a gentle hand towards him as the sound of her mother's heels clacking on the stone walkway receded into the house.

"I see you."

Her chest squeezed as his words hit her with full force. She gazed into his blue eyes, her heart turning to warm liquid sunshine in her chest. Here she was, a sweaty, dirty mess, with nothing to her name. Her own mother acted as if she didn't know her. But this man held her in his arms, holding her up when all she wanted to do was crumple to the ground. How could she not be falling for Turner?

20

———————

MADDY

"Let's go home." Turner walked Maddy to the truck and opened the passenger-side door for her. His hand steadied her waist as she climbed in.

"I'll load the mower and be right back. Get the air going." He handed her the keys and closed the door.

Maddy slipped off her work gloves and leaned across to start the truck as he had requested. She waited, staring out at her parents' front door. The curtain in the front of the house twitched. Maddy stared at that spot, numb.

"Was I really that much of a disappointment?" She laughed as Turner climbed into the truck.

His cautious gaze caught on her.

"It's just . . . I did everything they wanted. I kept the friends they wanted me to; I dated the boys they wanted me to. I did everything I could, and it was never enough. I was always an embarrassment to them."

Turner's hand gently landed on her thigh again. It was stained with grass and black oil. "They're idiots."

Maddy pulled down the mirror, studying her reflection.

Mud streaked her cheek where she'd tucked her hair behind her ear. She removed her hat and sunglasses to reveal matted sweat-soaked hair. More laughter poured from her. "Now look at me. Like an angel fallen from grace. Covered in dirt, doing manual labor, and stripping on the weekends. If they didn't accept me then, I can't imagine the disappointment I would be now." The humor in her voice died.

Turner shifted towards her. "You listen to me. You are a million times better as a mother than she'll ever be. You're a good woman who's been dealt a shitty hand." He jabbed his finger towards their luxurious home. "You fucking survived. Despite them. You proved me wrong ten times over. If I had any clue what it was really like for you back then, I'd . . ."

Maddy leaned over and kissed him. "Let's leave the past where it belongs. I think we've dredged it up enough. The reality is, I'm here now, and so are you." She turned back to the house, giving it one more lingering look. "I only wish Josh had more family than just me."

Turner slipped the truck into gear. "Geo sounded like he wanted to reconnect."

She smiled. "Probably thanks to Jasmine."

He drove out of the neighborhood, his hand never leaving her thigh. "You know, my dad is pretty fond of Josh. Who couldn't be? The kid is adorable."

"He is." Warmth spread through her chest.

"He's a good boy, and that doesn't happen by accident. You've done an amazing job raising him alone." Turner slipped his hand into hers.

"Thank you."

He lifted her knuckles to his lips and pressed his mouth there. His focus flicked to her eyes and then back to the road. "Thank you for giving me another chance."

"I should say the same."

Turner guided them through the town and back to the garage. The other truck was already parked there, which meant the other employees were done for the day too. Maddy slipped out of the truck and headed towards the house.

"What's that?" Turner asked.

Maddy stopped and spun around.

Turner walked over to her car and picked up a white envelope from under the windshield wiper. He held it out to her expectantly.

Her name was scratched on the front of it in a script she didn't recognize. She opened it and pulled out the contents—a grainy, dark photo of her dancing at the club, her head thrown back as she twisted her body around the pole. Maddy's brows drew together. Who would send her this? She flipped it over and all the blood drained from her face. The photograph trembled in her hands.

You think this is over between us? Not even close. I will get what I'm owed, one way or another.

"What the fuck is this?" Turner grabbed the picture from her hands. "Who would send this to you?"

Maddy shook her head. Was it Chris? Her stomach dropped. Her eyes began to race wildly over the street. Was someone watching her right now?

"We should take this to the police. Bently is sheriff now. He can help."

Maddy shook her head. Had Scott found out where she'd gone? "No."

"Why not?" he asked, setting both hands on her arms and studying her.

"Because I've been down this road before. They can't do anything. We don't know who sent it, and there isn't an explicit threat on it. Even if there was, at best I'd get a restraining order." *Unless it's Chris with his daddy's connections, in which case we'd have no chance.* How had she ended up back in this position?

"What do you mean you've done this before? Is this someone from your past?"

Maddy leaned into his arms, needing his strength for this next part. She sucked in a stuttered breath. Surely Turner would understand. *I need someone in my corner.* "Why do you think I'm working cash-paying jobs?"

"Are you hiding from someone?" His body tensed around her.

"Sort of." She pulled back. "The man who broke into my apartment had connections with the local police—his uncle was the chief. I got away, and I didn't think he'd follow me. But I was careful just in case . . . but it could be someone else."

"Who else would do this?"

"I had an . . . altercation with someone at the club last week."

Turner's body turned to steel. "Why didn't you tell me?"

"Because it happened right before you came in, and then we . . ."

Turner let out a frustrated sigh, taking off his ball cap and running his hands through his hair. "Jesus Christ."

Maddy tucked her arms across her chest, lowering her head. "I'm sorry I brought this to your door."

Turner's hands rested on her shoulders, his eyes boring into hers. "You better not think this is your fault."

"But—"

"But nothing. It's their fault for being entitled slimy dicks who can't get it into their tiny fucking brains that when a woman says 'no,' they have no right to her body." He let out a frustrated growl. "I hate this. I hate that you have to deal with this. You're done at the club."

"To hell I am!" she snapped. "I need that income."

"Maddy—"

She pressed her finger into his chest. "You listen here. You do not control my decisions. The club is safe. The bouncers walk us to our cars every evening, and there are strict rules of conduct. I wouldn't be there if it wasn't a necessity, but it is—and before you even think of telling me you can give me the money, don't. I won't be a charity case."

"I just want to protect you." Turner's voice cracked.

Her anger dissipated. She'd never had anyone who wanted to shield her from pain before. "Let's just wait and see what happens. This might be an empty threat."

"You'll tell me if it happens again?"

She nodded.

"I'll be driving you to the club and picking you up."

She opened her mouth to protest, but his unwavering gaze told her he wouldn't budge. That protectiveness of his brought a tightness to her chest. "Okay, but we stay in communication about this. It's my life, and I have the final say."

His jaw pulsed but he finally nodded in agreement. "Okay, princess."

She scrunched her nose up. "Why do you still call me that?"

He smirked. "Does it bother you?"

"It did. I just don't want you to view me as some spoiled helpless girl."

He chuckled and wrapped his arm around her, leading her into the house where they could both get the shower they so desperately needed. "It might have started out that way, but to me, you're someone who deserves to be spoiled and taken care of. And I aim to be the man to do that."

Another piece of her armor chipped away and fell just a little more for Turner. A small part of her wondered if that would be enough—if Turner could keep the ghosts of her past away—or if in the end, she'd lose everything due to the secrets she kept. Nothing stayed buried for forever.

TURNER

Turner entered Bently's office. Jasmine's older brother looked up from the paperwork on his desk, a friendly smile tipping the corners of his mouth up.

"Hey, T. How you been, man?" Bently shook Turner's hand.

Turner took a seat across from him. "Can't complain."

"You back for good?"

Turner nodded. "Yeah. Dad's retiring and I'm taking over the business."

"How's Stephanie?" Bently asked.

A pang of guilt flitted through his stomach. He hadn't told Maddy about her yet. "She's doing well."

"Glad to hear it. What can I do for you today?"

Turner produced the envelope to Bently and then sat back in his chair.

Bently pulled the photo out and studied it before flipping it over. "What's this?"

"You remember Maddy Miller?"

Bently's brows drew together. "She the girl who bullied my sister?"

Turner sighed and nodded. "Yeah, but she's . . ." How could he explain all of this? ". . . *changed*. Maddy was going through a lot back then. She's met up with Jaz recently and made amends."

Bently studied Turner. "Is she someone to you?"

Turner nodded. "We're dating."

Bently remained quiet for a few moments. "Any idea who sent the card?"

Turner's leg jiggled up and down. "What I tell you stays between us, right?"

"Not if you confess to a crime."

"It's nothing like that. It's more . . . let's say hypothetically I knew someone who had been raped."

Bently's face hardened and his back straightened. "Go on."

"And the attackers were two people with a lot of connections and money. There might even be evidence sitting in a storage container somewhere because of the power this family holds."

"Hypothetically, are we talking Holt kind of connections?" Bently asked, an edge to his tone.

Turner didn't want to betray Maddy's trust, but he also couldn't let this go. She needed his protection, and he'd do whatever it took so she and Josh could be safe. He had fucked up in high school, but he would never fail her again.

"You could say that."

"Do you have any proof?"

"I was thinking—what if I could get him admitting or threatening her on tape?"

Bently shook his head. "The Holts are not that stupid.

Besides, New Hampshire is a two-party consent state for recording."

Turner nodded, slumping in his seat.

"Nothing you record could be used in court. But—hypothetically, of course—a video like that might make front page news. Of course, the family would want to try to squash it by any means necessary, and that might involve dragging the victim through the mud."

Right. Turner hadn't thought of that. But if he had a recording, at least Maddy would have some form of protection against them. They might even back off and leave her alone.

"How much does this girl mean to you?" Bently asked.

"A lot." The confession fell from his lips before he thought better of it. He hadn't even told Maddy how much yet.

Bently's eyebrows rose before he nodded. "Sounds pretty complicated, with you still being married and all."

Turner's stomach sank like a rock. "You know Stephanie and I are over. Just waiting for the paperwork to sign and then it's officially done."

"Does Maddy know?"

He shook his head. "She's got enough to deal with right now. Steph and I have been over for more than a year—longer, actually. We finally got the nerve to file. I'm a signature away from everything being finalized."

"Well, take it from me—I learned the hard way with my wife. Keeping stuff from one another has a way of coming back to ruin things when you least expect it." Bently scratched the dark stubble on his chin.

"How is Belle these days?"

Bently smiled, his eyes lighting up at the mention of his wife's name. If Turner had been a betting man, he would have put money on Bently Evans never settling down—and he would have lost. Turner hadn't counted on a force to be reckoned with coming to Shattered Cove—but Belle had arrived, and she'd captured Bently's heart.

"She's great. Keeping busy between her shifts at the hospital and our foster teens." Bently flipped the photo on his desk around. His wife's beautiful face smiled brightly. Bently's arm was around her and the three teens who seemed to be laughing in the photo.

"That's great, man."

Bently set the frame back to facing him. "Thanks." He cleared his throat and looked directly at Turner. "I hope you know what you're doing."

"Me too."

Maddy's story was her own. But if he could get one of the Holts on video admitting to something, it might just be the leverage she needed to protect herself. Surely, she'd understand that.

22

———

MADDY

Maddy carried the laundry basket to the room she shared with Josh. Voices were coming from inside. She tipped her head and peeked through the crack in the door.

Turner sat on the bed by Josh's side. Her little boy was curled up, laying his head on Turner's side, both focused on the book the man was holding. Her heart squeezed. *I wish I had my phone to take a picture of this.* She stood there a moment longer, memorizing this snapshot.

"And both the princes lived happily ever after. The end." Turner closed the book.

"Wead it again!" Josh pleaded.

Turner chuckled.

Maddy opened the door and walked in. "No more stories for you, mister. It's time for bed."

"Awww. But me not sleepy," Josh protested as Turner got up from the bed and pulled the blankets over him.

"You know you gotta sleep if you want to grow bigger.

Most of your growing happens at night." Turner smiled down at her son.

Josh's sleepy eyes widened. "Weally?"

Turner nodded. "Absolutely. How do you think I got so big?"

"I wanna be big and strong like you. Night, Mommy. Night-night, TT."

Turner ruffled his hair. "Night, bud."

Maddy set the basket of clothes down and took Turner's place, laying a kiss on her son's head and curling her body around him. "I love you, little prince."

"Wuv you too, Mama." Josh yawned.

Turner left the room and shut the door with a snick.

"Sing me, Mama." Josh snuggled deeper into her side. She traced his profile with her finger, lightly running around his eyes and down his nose, and circling his mouth, then continuing over his whole face. The lyrics to "My Little Sunshine" fell from her lips as Josh's eyelashes fluttered closed and his breathing evened out. She stayed a few minutes extra, making sure he was asleep and savoring the sweet moment when her little ball of energy was still. She laid an extra kiss on his forehead and slipped out of bed, replacing her body with a pillow so he wouldn't roll off. She crept outside the door, shutting it as quietly as she could.

"You have thirty minutes to get dressed." Turner's voice from behind made her jump. His arms wrapped around her, pulling her into a hug.

"What do you mean? What's wrong with my pajamas?"

He pulled away, running his eyes down the length of her, heat igniting in his gaze. "Nothing, but I'm taking you out for a late dinner."

"But we already ate dinner," she reminded him.

"Dessert and drinks, then." He smiled mischievously. "My dad will take care of Josh."

His dad? Turner had planned this and set everything up in advance? "Where are we going?"

"You ask a lot of questions. It's a surprise. Go get dressed, and let me take you on a date."

"A date?" Her eyes flicked to his, widening.

His voice softened. "That's what boyfriends do—they take their girls on dates."

Boyfriend? They were making this official? Relief washed over her. Turner was showing her at every turn that he wasn't like the other men in her life who had used her and then gone on their way. He wanted more—a relationship.

"Okay," she agreed quietly, slipping back into her room to grab a cute summer dress and her toiletry bag.

She made her way to the bathroom, quickly changing out of her sleepwear and into the dress. She added some lilac perfume and pulled her hair into a ponytail. She focused on her face in the mirror. Makeup or not? Maybe just a little. This was her first date in five years, after all.

Forty-five minutes later, Turner opened the door for her, his hand resting possessively on her lower back as he guided her into Atlantis.

"Didn't this use to be the old fish store?" she asked, taking in the warm ambiance of the room. Low-hanging Edison lights hung over every dark-stained wooden table. Large black-and-white photographs hung on the walls, depicting fishermen with their catches and farmers in their fields. Some of the faces she recognized.

"Yup, Atlas bought it and converted it. He sources his food

from local fishermen and farmers whenever he can, so a lot of the menu is seasonal." Turner led them to the hostess.

The young girl smiled at them. "Good evening. Do you have a reservation?"

"Yes, Walker," Turner answered.

The hostess ran her finger over the iPad, tapped it, and then grabbed two menus. "Right this way."

They followed her towards the back of the restaurant, through a door and onto an outdoor porch. Candles in mason jars flickered on the tables, dancing in the sea air. The sound of water lapping in the bay below the deck melded into the background of other patrons' laughter and conversation.

Turner pulled out a chair and motioned for her to sit. Maddy took the seat and swallowed the ball of emotion that rose in her throat. *Is this real? Am I dreaming?*

Turner took the spot across from her, his handsome tan face even darker under the indigo sky. A few stars glittered overhead; the moon shone on the ocean to her left.

"This is beautiful," she said.

"Sure is," Turner agreed.

She turned back to catch his gaze focused on her.

"Can I get you drinks to start?" the hostess asked.

"I'll have a Sand Dune Summer IPA," Turner answered, without looking away from Maddy.

"Uh, I'll have a . . ." It had been ages since she'd had a drink, let alone been out. "A mojito, please." She fell back on one of her favorite cocktails.

"They'll be right out, and so will your server." The hostess left them.

"Didn't take you for a rum kinda girl," Turner noted.

Maddy leaned back in the comfortable chair and shrugged. "Thought I only drank champagne, huh?"

He chuckled. "I thought for sure white wine."

She shook her head. "God, no. Unless it's sweet. I like the mint and lime together."

He nodded.

She cast a glance at the door to the restaurant. "I can't believe how different things are now."

"You've been gone a long time."

She blinked and focused back on her menu, skimming the desserts. "By the way, who is Atlas?"

"Jasmine's husband."

Maddy's attention darted back to Turner. "Really?"

He nodded. "Yup."

"Her daughter is older than Josh." She tried to do the math. Either they'd reconnected after a long time apart or Atlas wasn't Zoey's father.

Turner leaned in, resting his elbows on the table. "Jasmine was a single mom for about four years or so. She got pregnant from a one-night stand and didn't know the man's name. Then two years ago, Atlas walked into her inn—it's down the road." He motioned over his shoulder.

"So they reconnected?"

He smirked. "Sort of."

Why did she feel like there was a much bigger story there?

"Here you are." A young man set their drinks in front of them. "I'm Will, and I'll be your server tonight. Have you had a chance to look at the menu, or would you like to hear our specials?"

"You know what you want?" Turner asked Maddy.

"The chocolate peanut butter cheesecake sounds delicious." She handed the menu to the server.

"I'll have the strawberry shortcake," Turner added.

The server took his menu. "They'll be right out."

Maddy waited until he was out of earshot before she spoke. "Thank you for this."

Turner reached across the table and threaded his fingers through hers. "Thank you for coming out with me."

"You said earlier that you were my boyfriend." She needed to be clear and make sure they were on the same page. She didn't want to have to second-guess anything. They'd had enough misunderstandings.

Turner leaned forward. "If you thought what happened between us was a one-time, casual thing, you'd be mistaken. I don't want pieces of you, princess. I want all of you. I want to be there for you and Josh as someone you can both rely on."

Her eyes stung with tears. His words struck her, stealing the breath from her lungs. He was saying everything she'd wanted to hear for so long. "I want that too."

Those bright blue eyes beamed at her before he pulled her hand to his mouth and softly kissed it. "Best news I've had in a long time."

Her heart fluttered and dipped. He was choosing her.

The warm joy bubbling in her chest suddenly turned cold. The tiny hairs on her neck stood on end as a shiver zipped through her. It was as if someone was watching her. She turned, scanning the other patrons in the outdoor seating. A few glanced her way, but she didn't recognize any of them.

Did she and Turner really get a second chance after all? Or would her past hold her prisoner?

23

TURNER

Turner held Maddy's hand as he led her through the dark house, careful not to wake his dad or her sleeping son. He knocked into a lamp, quickly grabbing it before it could fall.

Maddy clapped a hand over her mouth, but a giggle escaped. He grinned. It was like he was back in high school, trying to sneak a girl in his room, but he was no boy—and Maddy was certainly all woman now.

"Sshhh." He tried not to laugh too loudly himself as he continued guiding her up the stairs.

She tugged his hand, halting him. "Wait."

He turned to her, the moonlight sparkling in her eyes. "What is it?"

"I don't want this night to end just yet." Her voice was all breath.

He'd been fighting a hard-on since she'd walked out of the bathroom in that sweet pink sundress. He'd been trying to keep his arousal in check. The last thing he wanted was to ruin things again and have her thinking all he wanted was sex.

"Come on." He gripped her hand and led her back down the stairs and out the front door to his garage. He flicked on only one of the lights, keeping the room light enough to see her, but not enough to illuminate the whole room.

She looked around the space. It smelled like engine oil and metal in here. Her sweet floral scent was in stark contrast. He loved it.

"You wanna talk some more?" he asked. Over dessert, he'd discovered she wasn't sure exactly what she wanted to do with her life in the future, but accounting wasn't out of the question. She liked doing his dad's bookkeeping. She hadn't thought about much more than survival these past several years. Mostly, they'd talked about Josh—funny moments in his life, and the challenges of her raising him on her own.

"No, I don't want to talk." She slipped her hand over his chest, her big doe eyes locked on his.

"You want to kiss me?"

She nodded, biting her bottom lip. "I want to do so many things to you."

He swallowed, his cock turning to steel. "We don't have to."

She stepped closer so that her hard nipples rubbed against his chest through the thin fabric of her cotton dress. "And that's why I want to."

He raised his hand to trace her jaw with his thumb. His control was hanging on by a thread. He wanted to order her to strip, but hesitation bled through the space between them. Because of her past, shouldn't he be more careful with her? Images of her spanking the other dancer flashed through his mind. "You want to be in control of this, princess?"

She shook her head. "No. I want you to be. I don't want to think or have to choose anything. I'm all yours. Tell me what to do."

"Fuck, that's the sexiest thing you could have said." His chest heaved.

She raised one lone eyebrow as if in challenge. "I could think of a lot of other things that might be dirtier."

"I believe that, but nothing will ever compare to you handing over your trust like this."

She blinked, her eyes widening for a fraction of a second. Had she even realized what she'd done? "I . . . I do trust you."

His mouth crashed against hers. His hands cupped her face. Tiny whimpers filled the garage. He threaded his fingers through the hair at the base of her skull and tugged, exposing her neck to him. He kissed and sucked under her jaw, moving down. She swallowed, her delicate throat bobbing. Turner raked his teeth over the curve where her shoulder met her neck. She gasped, hands tearing at his shirt. He licked the same spot, mixing up the sensations for her.

"Turner." His name was a plea on her lips.

"I'm just getting started, sweetheart. Gonna have to be patient."

She let out a frustrated mewl as he lowered the straps of her dress, kissing and nipping all around her exposed breasts, teasing and tempting her before he slipped one nipple into his mouth, sucking.

"Oh, God."

He massaged her other tit, pinching the nipple between his fingers. She shuddered, grasping his head, raking her fingernails over his scalp.

Turner lowered one of his hands, skimming her skin and then gripping her ass.

"Please?" she asked.

"What do you need, princess?"

"Touch me."

"You gotta be more specific than that." He gave a dark

chuckle before tugging her nipple with his teeth.

She sucked in a breath, her breath coming in short pants. "My clit. Touch my clit."

He backed away, releasing her and flicking open the top buttons on his shirt before pulling it over his head and tossing it on the counter. "I'm the one in control, remember?"

She nodded as he undid his pants, letting them fall to the ground and then stepping out. Maddy's eyes focused on his body, roaming down his wide shoulders and getting stuck on his abs. Lust clouded her blue gaze; it only made his dick harder.

"If you want me to stop, just say so, beautiful. Okay?"

She licked her kiss-swollen lips and nodded. Her dress hung at her waist, still exposing her breasts. He wanted all of her. But first, he'd drive her mad with desire so that when she broke apart, it would be bigger than the fireworks finale on the Fourth of July.

He tugged off his boxer briefs, his cock bouncing towards his stomach. Grabbing the shaft, he ran his hand over it and squeezed. She licked her lips, staring at his dick.

"You're gonna make me come if you keep looking at me like that," he growled.

"I'd much rather make you come in my mouth," she teased.

His hand wrapped around her throat, applying gentle pressure to the sides of her neck on the artery.

Maddy's eyes widened as he backed her up against the wall. He leaned down to her ear. "You'll get your chance to suck my cock. But not until I tell you. Understand?"

"Yes."

He leaned back to study her reaction. Was she into this? Or was he taking things too far?

"I'm not made of glass. What now?" she asked, seeming to

sense his hesitation.

"Now, you're gonna stand here while I finger your pussy until you come like a good girl."

Her exhale was ragged as if she were barely hanging on. Anticipation wound through the air, thick and heady. Her arousal permeated the room, intoxicating him. His hand slid up her thigh, lifting the hem of her dress. He cupped her sex. Maddy gripped his arms as if steadying herself.

He tugged at the scrap of lace that she called panties, tearing them off her. She gasped, her eyes darkening until they were almost black.

His mouth rested against the shell of her ear as his fingers slipped inside her tight hole. She trembled, her chest rising faster and faster as he worked another finger inside. Moans and whimpers fell from her lips like explicit lyrics in an erotic melody.

"You're so fucking wet. Your pussy takes my fingers like the greedy cunt it is." He pulled back, studying her reaction. Her eyes rolled up, her body tensing as she arched from the wall, liquid arousal gushing over his hand. He smiled. She was fucking perfect.

"Can you handle me, sweetheart?"

Hazy eyes landed on his. "More. Give me more. All of it. I want . . ."

"You want what?"

"Everything."

"You like when I talk dirty to you?" He curled his fingers, pressing against her swollen G-spot.

She nodded, tipping her head back, thrusting her breasts out.

He leaned down, sucking one into his mouth, gently licking. In contrast, he thrust his fingers faster inside her, making sure to hit that spongy spot inside each time.

"Oh, God. Fuck! I'm gonna come," Maddy cried.

"Not yet." He withdrew his fingers from her, slipping them inside her mouth before she could protest.

Lust-fueled eyes locked on his. "You'll come when I tell you to. And I'm gonna feel it on my cock."

He bent down and grabbed the foil wrapper from the pocket of his discarded pants. He handed it over to her. "Put it on me."

She snatched the condom, ripped the package open and dropped to her knees. She slipped her hot, wet mouth over his cock, and he groaned.

"Fuuuuuuck."

She sucked, swirling her tongue like a goddamned fantasy come to life.

"You bad girl. You didn't follow the rules," he ground out, pleasure tingling down his spine as she sucked his remaining restraint from his body.

She licked the tip, sitting back to slide the latex on before she looked up at him. "Are you gonna punish me?"

The last thread of his control snapped. He gripped the back of her neck, pulling her to her feet as his mouth slanted against hers. His hands fell to her ass, slapping both sides. She gasped, but he swallowed her cry. His palms skidded up her dress, his fingers digging into her hips as he lifted her and pinned her against the wall once more. Her fingernails dug tiny half-moons of pain into his shoulders; she clung to him as if her life depended on it. He lined the tip of his cock up with her pussy and drove into her. They collided, sucking the air from his lungs. His eyes were wide; color sharpened. His senses were enveloped with ecstasy.

"You're so tight," he gritted out, moving faster and faster. Her breasts bounced with each drive of his hips.

"Yes! Turner. Yes," Maddy keened.

Pleasure gathered at the base of his spine, pressure building as his balls drew up. He slipped a hand between them, pressing his thumb to her clit. "Come for me, like a good girl. Let go and come," he commanded.

He kissed her, swallowing her cries as her body convulsed, tensing around him. Her orgasm shuddered through her. Her eyes rolled back, her hair was mussed, and pure ecstasy was painted on her face. It was the most beautiful thing he'd ever seen.

His orgasm came charging like a bull, slamming through him. He jerked and pulsed inside her, his hot cum shooting into the condom.

"Maddy!" he roared her name.

His thrusts slowed, the sound of their breathing coming back to him. He kissed her gently, drawing out the moment just a little longer before he set her on her feet and slid out of her.

Cupping her face in his hands, he searched her for any sign of distress. Glazed eyes, hazy from pleasure, reflected back at him. Her features relaxed into a contented expression. "You okay?"

She gave him a lazy smile. "Better than okay."

Relief loosened his chest. "That wasn't too much?"

She shook her head. "That was fucking hot. I've never felt so . . . so beautiful."

His eyebrows drew together. How could this precious woman ever doubt she was anything less than perfection? He'd do whatever he had to in order to make sure she felt this way every day for the rest of her life. Because Maddy Miller was his.

Oh my God.

I love her.

24

TURNER

Turner opened his eyes, wincing at the bright light filtering in through the window. He rolled over, searching for any sign of the woman whose perfume lingered on his pillow. He grabbed his phone and scrolled through his e-mail. A Google alert caught his eye. He clicked on the link and read the article. It seemed Chris and Brett Holt would be in the city at a political event later that afternoon. His stomach churned and bile rose in his throat at the sight of their smiling faces. Anger blistered his insides. *They deserve to pay for what they did to Maddy.*

A giggle erupted from across the hall. Turner smiled and got out of bed, then took a detour to the bathroom to brush his teeth, relieve himself, and calm down before knocking on Maddy and Josh's door.

"Come in," Maddy's sweet voice answered before another bout of little-boy giggles erupted.

Turner opened the door and leaned against the frame, taking in the scene before him. Maddy sat on the ground, her back to the dresser, surrounded by a pile of scattered clothes.

Josh lay in her lap, gazing up at his mother with so much affection, like Maddy was the center of his world. Maddy folded one of his shirts and laid it in the pile, and then came back to tickle his belly. Josh laughed.

"Again." He grinned.

Maddy caught Turner's gaze and smiled, a slight blush coming to her cheeks before she reached for another item of clothing and repeated the process.

"Good morning, beautiful," Turner greeted.

The pink on Maddy's cheeks turned to red. The woman could dance almost naked in front of a crowd but compliments made her self-conscious?

"Morning," she replied without looking him in the eye.

"You think Mama is boo-ti-ful?" Josh asked, sitting up and climbing out of her lap to stand in front of Turner.

"I sure do."

"Me too." Josh smiled, his eyes lighting up. "Papa Walker is taking me fishing."

Turner's mouth dropped open in exaggerated surprise. "He is? You're so lucky."

"Me gonna catch a big fish." Josh held out his hands as far as they could go.

Turner's eyes widened. "Whoa. I bet you will. Papa Walker knows all the best places."

"Are you comin'?" Josh asked clapping his hands together and jumping up and down.

"No, I'm gonna stay here and keep your mom company so she isn't lonely." Turner winked at Maddy.

"Oh, otay."

"Ready to go, little guy?" his dad called from the bottom of the stairs.

"Yes!" Josh ran out of the room.

"Hey—" Maddy started to protest but Josh returned,

running into her and wrapping his little arms around her neck.

"Bye-bye, Mommy."

She squeezed him tight and kissed his cheek. "Listen to Papa Walker and keep your life jacket on. I packed your snacks and drinks in your backpack. And have fun."

"Luv you."

"Love you too."

Josh grabbed his leg and hugged it. "Bye, TT."

"See ya later, buddy."

Josh took off. His dad's voice mixing with the little boy's for a few moments until they were gone.

Turner came inside and sat across from her on the floor, the bed to his back. He picked up a pair of Josh's pants and folded them.

"You don't have to do this." Maddy picked up another item, repeating the process.

He didn't mind it at all. Just being in her presence brought a lightness to his chest. "I know. But the sooner you get done with this, the sooner I can take you back to bed."

Her eyebrows rose. "Oh, you think it will be that easy, huh?"

He shrugged and picked up a pair of her panties, waggling his eyebrows. "You seemed to be pretty eager last night."

She grabbed them from him and shook her head, a small smile playing on the corners of her mouth. "You are incorrigible."

"Fancy words from the princess. I shouldn't have expected less." He chuckled.

She rolled her eyes and folded the last piece of clothing, then added it to the pile. "I have things to do today, you know."

He crawled forward, nuzzling her neck, and then kissing a trail over her jaw. "Like what?"

Her breath hitched as he sucked on the sensitive spot behind her ear. "I'm meeting Jasmine, actually, for lunch."

He pulled back. "Really?"

She nodded shyly. "Yeah, she wanted to introduce me to her sisters-in-law. We're gonna meet at The Stardust Café and carpool together into the city."

Turner sat back on his heels, taking in the woman across from him. How could he ever have doubted her intentions?

"Does that bother you?" Maddy asked.

He shook his head. "No. I'm happy you and her are getting along."

Maddy's shoulders relaxed on an exhale, like she was relieved.

"What time do you have to leave?"

She smiled. "Eleven."

Turner made a show of glancing at his watch. "That means we still have a couple hours to make the most of."

"Can't get enough of me, Mister Walker?" she teased.

He crawled back over to her, laying a sweet kiss on her lips, taking his time to coax her tongue with his. Her hands rested on his shoulders, pulling him closer as he deepened the kiss. Turner leaned back enough to lock eyes with her. "I don't think I'll ever get enough of you, princess."

She blinked, vulnerability flashing in her blue gaze. "I hope you mean that."

"I do." He gently cupped her face in his hands. She leaned into him, closing her eyes. So fragile and perfect—this woman was a gift. Gifts were to be cherished . . . and loved.

And that meant Turner would do whatever it took to keep her safe, even if it meant facing the devil himself—or, in this case, two.

25

TURNER

Turner tugged the collar of his shirt away from his neck and cleared his throat. Sweat beaded on his forehead as his nerves raced. His phone was ready in his pocket, set to record. He'd chosen a spot at the bar, figuring once the handshaking was done, they'd come here for a drink. It would look less suspicious if they approached him.

Turner lifted his glass, sipping the amber liquid slowly. He wished he could down the drink to calm his anxiety, but he needed his wits about him.

Deep, boisterous laughter came from the other side of the room, setting Turner's nerves on edge. *This is for Maddy. She needs some form of leverage to keep these slimy fucks away from her.*

A body moved beside him, taking the empty seat a couple of stools down. Turner risked a glance. *Brett.* Turner's stomach revolted, and it took everything in him not to fly out of his seat and beat the man into a bloody pulp. His knuckles whitened around the glass as he took a shaky breath. *It's now or never.*

Turner pretended to do a double take as Brett ordered a drink from the bartender. "Hey, I know you, don't I?"

Brett cast a critical eye over him, squinting before plastering a slick smile on his face. "You've just probably seen my face on TV."

"You sure we didn't go to high school together? Brett, right?"

Brett gave him another long stare.

"Turner Walker."

Recognition sparked in Brett's eyes. "Oh, yeah. How are you doing, man?"

The bartender placed a glass with clear liquid in front of Brett. He took a sip.

"Can't complain. Just got out of the Navy."

"No shit." Brett nodded.

"Yeah. It's weird being back. Running into everyone I used to know from school. Those were some good times, am I right?" Turner forced a smile, calling on his self-control to not snap the other man's neck.

"They were," Brett agreed, turning back towards the crowd like he was ready to leave.

"You were prom king, weren't you?" Turner asked, already knowing the answer.

Brett's chest puffed out as his smile deepened. "What can I say? I was just as popular back then as I am now."

"Yeah." Turner forced a chuckle. "You went with . . . oh, what was her name?" He'd left the door open—now all he had to do was reel him in.

"Madeline Miller." Brett's smirk deepened before he took another drink.

"She was a hottie. I always wanted to hit that, but she was an ice queen." The lies tasted like acid falling from Turner's mouth.

Brett drained the rest of his drink, signaling to the bartender for another. He moved to the seat next to Turner, his aftershave overpowering. Turner winced but forced himself to lean in as Brett did the same. This could be it. The moment he was here for.

"Girls like that just need a little something to loosen them up."

Motherfucker. "Like what?"

Brett shrugged and gave him a wink. "Whatever works."

Shit. If he pressed it, Brett would know something was off. But this was his only shot. "She wasn't much of a drinker in high school, was she?"

Brett paused, studying him a moment. Whatever war he waged in his head was won by his arrogance. "No, she wasn't. But that's when—"

"There you are, cousin." Chris Holt slapped Brett's shoulder, casting an inquisitive glance Turner's way. He grimaced like he'd found Turner wanting.

"Hey, Chris, you remember Turner Walker?" Brett asked.

Chris didn't even glance his way and waved the barkeep over. "Can't say that I do."

"He was at prom. Who'd you take as your date?" Brett asked.

Chris's attention snapped to Turner, eyeing him more closely. Turner forced what he hoped was an easy smile back on his face. "No one, really." He didn't need to remind these two of Jasmine's existence.

"You were at the after-party, right? But the prom queen never showed."

Chris's beady eyes sharpened as an evil smirk curved his mouth upwards. "That little slut? No, she fucked both of us in the back of a limo. Begged us for it. Said it was a fantasy of hers. Who were we to turn her down?"

What was left of his self-control snapped. Turner's hands flew around Chris's throat. The grin on the man's face only deepened.

"You slimy fuck! You raped her," Turner roared.

Someone nearby gasped.

"Get the fuck off him." Brett pulled at Turner's wrist as two beefy security men came running to the room. They each grabbed one of his arms, tugging him away from Chris, who straightened his jacket and offered a fake smile to the onlookers, holding up his hands. "Nothing to see here, folks. Just a drunken misunderstanding."

"The fuck it is! Admit it. Admit what you did to her!" Turner yelled, fighting the hold of the guards.

Chris leaned in, Brett at his side. "The truth is, she asked for it. Anything else is a lie. She's a stripper, for God's sake. No one will ever believe her word over mine. And if you ever embarrass me like this again, I will take . . . legal action." It was like the asshole knew he was being recorded. Each word was careful and rehearsed.

"You won't get away with this," Turner spat.

Chris beamed. "I already did."

Brett nodded to the guards. "Take the trash out, fellas."

"You better stay away from her!" Turner thrashed, fighting to get free. He just needed one good punch to wipe the condescending smile from that fucker's mouth.

One of the security guards jabbed him in the stomach, stealing his breath before they dragged him towards the back door. They launched him out onto the hard concrete. Pain radiated from his shoulder.

He reached into his pocket and grabbed the phone, praying he'd got all of it. The numbers were still going. He sighed in relief and pressed the stop button. He quickly sent a copy to Bently's e-mail and scrambled to his feet. He needed to get back to Shattered Cove.

Dialing his friend, he ran to his truck.

"Hello?" Bently answered.

"Check your e-mail. Tell me I got something we can use to hold over their heads."

Because if he didn't, this had all been for nothing.

"What did you do, Turner?" Bently's voice hardened.

"I got them on record. Tell me I have enough evidence to give her some leverage." He opened his truck and got in before sliding the key into the ignition.

Bently sighed. "Christ, you spoke to them?"

"I had to do something."

After a beat of silence, Bently responded, "I get it. I want to catch these scumbags, too, but that won't be admissible in court. They didn't agree to be recorded."

"Just check it over and let me know if I got anything," Turner pleaded.

"Fine. Give me an hour."

"I'll be there in thirty minutes." Turner shifted the car into gear and ended the call.

He raked a hand through his hair and let out a frustrated yell. "God dammit!" He needed this to work. Because how else could he keep the woman he loved safe?

26

MADDY

Maddy pressed her hand to her stomach. The muscles ached from laughing so hard. "I can't believe Zoey said that."

Jasmine shrugged with a smile. "She's my daughter, that's for sure. No filter, at all."

"Josh has had his moments too." Maddy grinned and looked out the car window as Jasmine pulled into the driveway to Gerry's house.

Jasmine put the vehicle in park. "I'm glad you could come with me today. It's nice to get away occasionally without the kids interrupting the conversation."

Maddy turned towards her. They'd shared an afternoon of lunch and shopping, laughter and conversation.

"I really appreciate the invite. It means a lot. Especially after everything I did to you in school. I truly regret how I treated you," Maddy apologized again.

Jasmine nodded. "I know. Thank you for saying so. I'm ready to leave the past where it belongs and move forward. I'd love it if we could be friends?"

"Absolutely," Maddy readily agreed. Maddy wasn't used to having friends, and she never in a million years would have thought that was what Jasmine would become to her, but after today, she had hope.

"Don't forget your things." Jasmine pointed to the bag in the back seat.

"Josh is going to love the new toy." Maddy grabbed the handle and pulled it into her lap before reaching for the door.

She exited the car and waved to Jasmine. Her friend drove off. Maddy headed towards the house. Gerry's car was gone, which meant Josh was still fishing. She tipped her head back, enjoying the warm sunshine on her face. Birds sang from the trees, and a light breeze blew her sundress gently around her knees. Happiness radiated through her. For the first time in a long time, she was at peace. No, things were not perfect, but that was life. She dug her phone from her pocket and shot off a text to Turner.

Maddy: *I'm back and your dad is still out with Josh. We should take advantage of the empty house. When will you be here?*

Bubbles appeared immediately.

Turner: *I'll be home in ten minutes.*

Maddy smiled. She liked the way he said *home*. Gerry's house was the only place she'd ever had that restful feeling of contentment. Staying here was like being part of a family, like she'd envied others for having for so long.

Maddy continued down the path. She reached for the doorknob and froze. An envelope with her name on it was tucked between the screen and main door. She turned, her senses on alert as her eyes darted to the street behind her. A neighbor was out mowing the lawn. A few cars drove by, but nothing else seemed amiss.

Is this another threat?

She picked it up, then slid her key into the front door and

quickly dashed inside before locking up behind her. She set the bag of things she'd bought on the floor by the door and ripped open the envelope as she walked into the kitchen. Dumping the contents of the envelope onto the table, she held her breath. Nerves and uncertainty writhed inside her stomach. Nothing could have prepared her for this.

Color images of Turner having drinks with the two men who'd assaulted her. Turner smiling and laughing with them.

"This doesn't make any sense." Her eyes scanned the photos again, bile rising up her throat. Her hands trembled, her heart racing. Why would he do that? She wouldn't have believed it, except she was seeing it with her own two eyes.

A car door shutting outside made her jump. She stuffed the photos back in the envelope and ran to slide it into the bag by the door. She stepped back as a key jiggled in the door, and Turner opened it.

He walked in, and the color drained from her face. He was wearing the exact same clothes he'd had on in the photographs—a navy-blue suit and white dress shirt unbuttoned at the top, and a shiny pair of dress shoes.

"Maddy? What's wrong?" Turner's voice brought her attention back to his face.

His eyes were narrowed in concern, alert and trained on her.

"Where were you today?"

His eyes flashed with guilt as they darted to the floor and back to her. "Had some errands to run."

He wasn't even going to tell her the truth? Had she really read him entirely wrong? She dug into the bag and threw the envelope at his chest. He caught it, his eyebrows drawing together. He had the audacity to seem confused.

"Did someone leave you another message?" He ripped open the paper as all the color leeched from his face. He turned his pleading eyes to her. "I can explain." Turner reached out to her, but she jerked away, shaking her head.

Anger swelled in her gut, pressure building until it erupted like a volcano. Her stomach roiled in disgust, and she cried hot tears of fury. "Don't fucking touch me!"

Maddy spun around and ran upstairs to her room. She shut the door and locked herself in, falling against the wooden panel. She dropped the bag with things for Josh and curled into a ball as sobs wracked her body.

How could he? There's no way I can stay now.

"Maddy? Princess, let me explain. Please?" Turner's soft voice filtered through the door.

She bit down on her lip, trying to quiet her crying. Her eyes stung. Her chest ached as if someone had shot a cannonball at it.

"You know me, Maddy. You know I wouldn't do anything to hurt you. Don't you?" Turner asked.

Did she? She'd thought so, but those pictures made her question everything.

"Deep down, you know I'd never meet with those kinds of guys unless I had a purpose."

She sniffed and stood. Wiping her eyes, she inhaled a shaky breath. "Then why?"

He sighed. "It would be easier if I could see your face while we talked."

She couldn't hide from those eyes forever. Maddy swallowed and unlocked the door. Turner twisted the handle a moment later and stepped inside. She backed up a few steps and crossed her arms.

Sadness filled his blue gaze. "I saw they were going to be in the city, and I thought if I could get them on a recording device admitting to something, you'd have evidence to hold against them so they would leave you alone."

She blinked, not sure she was hearing him correctly.

"It took everything in me not to beat the fuckers right there and then. And I should have. What those photos don't show is me trying to strangle Chris and being carried out by their two lug-head bodyguards."

She shook her head, scanning him more closely. One button was missing from his dress shirt near a stain that appeared to be dirt. His suit was rumpled, and Turner's hair was disheveled, like he'd run his hands through it many times.

"I was trying to fix it," Turner confessed. "I managed to fuck it up even more. I got nothing on the recording, and it wasn't even admissible. Bently said it wasn't enough."

"You got Bently involved in this?" she hissed.

He winced. "I was trying to help protect you."

"Newsflash: I've been taking care of myself for as long as I can remember. I don't need you to try and fix things for me like I'm some helpless girl. I can't believe you didn't even talk to me about this. You just acted on your own, thinking you knew what was best for me, like I'm a child." She shook her head.

"I'm sorry. I won't do it again."

"I can save myself. I've been doing it my entire life." Her voice cracked with emotion.

"You're right. I should have spoken to you and gotten your permission. I won't do it again."

Her eyebrows rose. "You think you'll have another opportunity?"

His expression softened as he hung his head. Turner's shoulders slumped in defeat. When he looked back up at her, his eyes were red and glassy with unshed tears. "Please give me another chance. I really only had the best intentions. I went about it entirely the wrong way—I fully admit that. I couldn't bear to lose you."

His words tugged at her heart. Her chest cinched tight. Hope bubbled inside her. "Why?"

Slowly, Turner stepped closer and reached his hand to her face, dragging his knuckle across her jaw. She closed her eyes momentarily, drinking in the familiar buzz of energy thrumming through her from their connection. She met his gaze, intent and vulnerable, like he was trying to let her see everything inside him.

"Because I love you, princess."

Love? She gasped.

His thumb brushed her cheek as he moved closer still until his chest met hers. His other hand gently tipped her focus towards him. "I love you, Maddy, and I can't see my future without you by my side, and little Josh."

Tears sprung from her eyes once more. Was this real? Or was she dreaming? "If you truly love me, you won't lie to me again. I can't live with any more secrets. Promise you won't repeat something like this. That you'll tell me the honest truth even when you think I won't like it."

Hesitation flashed in his gaze before he nodded. "I promise."

He leaned the rest of the way until his lips pressed against hers. The kiss was slow and full of penitence. An apology of lips and tongues. She relaxed into his embrace, taking all that he had to give.

The doorbell rang; she pulled away. Her chest heaved. His fingers swiped the tears from her face and then he kissed her cheeks. "I'm sorry for hurting you. That was the last thing I wanted."

She nodded. "I know."

"Do you?"

"Yes." And she meant it. She knew it in her heart; Turner was a good man.

"I better go see who that is. How about I cook you dinner tonight?" He backed away to the door.

She followed. "You can cook?"

He gave her a silly grin. "Just you wait and see, princess."

She laughed as he went downstairs. The front door slammed shut as she reached the foot of the stairs. Turner held up another envelope, all humor gone from his expression.

"Another one?" She moved closer, afraid to look but needing to know at the same time.

"It just has your name on it." Turner tore open the top before pulling the contents out. More photographs, only this time it was Maddy with Jasmine in the city. Maddy and Josh around town this past week. Maddy and Turner at the park with her son.

A single slip of scratchy handwriting rested underneath the pile.

You've been a bad girl, Maddy. And your time is running out.

"That's it. We need to call Bently. I've already filled him in on the basics because of what I tried to do today. Please?" Turner begged.

"Do it." Maddy nodded, unable to tear her gaze from the image of Josh smiling up at her in the photo.

No one messed with her kid and got away with it. She'd raise hell on earth, burn the whole city to the ground if she had to in order to protect Josh.

It was time for the mama bear in her to show its claws.

27

MADDY

Maddy stared at the headline on her phone. Her rapist was running for city council. Her stomach churned with disgust and roiled with righteous anger. *Maybe I should have reported what they did to me back then.* But who would have listened? *I wouldn't have even had my parents on my side.* Any lawyer the state would have provided for her would have been no match for the Holts' army of sharks.

She closed the news app and sighed, turning towards her son who was happily kicking the soccer ball in the backyard. *Is there something I can do now? Are they stalking me and sending the messages?* Could she stay in a town where the people thought so highly of her attackers?

"Mommy, watch!" Josh yelled from across the yard.

She smiled and waved at him. "I'm watching."

He kicked nothing but air and then tried again. This time, he hit the black-and-white ball sending it towards the goal on the other side of the yard. He ran towards it, repeating the action three times before he made it into the goal.

"Yay! You did it. Awesome job." Maddy clapped and cheered for him.

Josh beamed.

"Hey, guys." Turner's voice pulled her attention to the back door. He walked out in a short-sleeve shirt that was snug enough to show off his wide shoulders and defined muscles. His tan skin had darkened in the summer sun. He was almost the same shade as his father after less than two months at home. Those blue eyes and curly blond hair contrasted against his skin.

"Hey yourself." Maddy smiled.

"TT!" Josh yelled and ran straight into Turner's legs.

Turner pretended to fall, lying on the grass. "Whoa, you knocked me right over, little man. You're so strong. You must be the Hulk."

Josh beamed, his eyes sparkling as his little chest puffed out. "I'm not the green guy; I'm the Black Panther. Rawrr!" Josh crooked his fingers like claws and growled, sounding more like a kitten than a ferocious wildcat.

Turner's eyes widened in feigned shock. "Whoa. I had no idea I was in the presence of royalty. I had heard that panthers liked to have their tummies rubbed like big kitties. You think you'd like that?"

Josh lay on the grass beside him. "Yeah!"

Turner reached over and started tickling his belly. Josh giggled. Every now and then, Turner would let up and ask if Josh wanted him to keep going. Josh lapped up the attention. Affection flit through Maddy's chest as she witnessed the two of them having fun together. Grateful, happy tears burned the back of her eyes. She'd wanted Josh to have a man in his life for so long, and now he had two. Maddy had given up that dream, along with many others. But it seemed that maybe she'd get her wish after all.

"Alright, that's enough. I think the Black Panther needs a rest." Turner sat up.

Josh crawled behind him, jumping onto his back and wrapping his little arms around Turner's wide neck. Turner wrapped one arm behind him, holding the young boy securely on his back before he rose to his feet.

"Crap. I think I lost Josh. Have you seen him?" Turner asked Maddy, spinning in a circle.

Josh giggled behind him.

"I can hear him, but I can't find him," Turner joked.

Maddy stood and made her way over to them in the lush green grass. "He was just here. He has to be close."

"I'm right here, Mommy!" Josh exclaimed, laughing.

"Oh, there you are. I thought we lost you." Her eyes locked on Turner's, which were so full of joy and contentment. So completely filled with love, and it was all aimed at her.

"I love you too," she said before reaching up on tiptoes and planting a kiss on his stunned lips. His free arm wrapped around her waist, drawing her closer.

"Ewww." Josh interrupted their moment.

Maddy laughed and Turner joined her.

"Why you kiss my mommy, TT?" Josh asked.

Turner smiled at her. "Because she's amazing."

"Do you want some kisses too?" Maddy asked Josh, walking around to pepper them on his arms and cheek.

"Stop, Mommy. Is too much kisses." He giggled.

Maddy backed up. "All right."

"What would you two say about taking a trip to town? We can go to The Oyster Bookstore and see if they have anything new for bedtime, and then maybe get some treats across the street from The Stardust Café."

"And ice cream." Josh wiggled off Turner's back.

Turner chuckled. "How about ice cream after lunch at Pirates Pizzeria?"

Josh crossed his arms and pursed his little lips. "Otay. But I gets two scoops." Josh held out three fingers.

Turner smiled. "I think we could swing that if your mom says it's okay."

Josh turned to Maddy, giving her his puppy-dog-eyed look, sticking his bottom lip out. "Pease, Mommy? I eat all my pizza first."

"I guess so."

"Yay! I go gets my toy to bring with me. Black Panther hasn't been to the bookstore." He ran into the house, the screen door slamming shut behind him.

Turner's hands wrapped around Maddy's waist, drawing her back against his front. His scratchy beard rested in the crook of her neck, sending shivers down her body as goose-flesh pricked her skin.

"Thank you for being so good to him, to us."

Turner kissed her cheek, his breath hot against her ear. "I'd do anything for you and Joshua. I love you both."

Emotion blocked her throat, and she swallowed it down. She turned to face him, hooking her arms around his neck as she stared into those bottomless eyes. "How did I get so lucky?"

His chest rumbled with his chuckle, as he nuzzled her cheek with his nose. "I'm the lucky one, princess."

He kissed her, tenderly. His arms wrapped around her, his actions full of protection and love. If she could freeze several key moments to relive over and over, this would be one of them. Pure contentment flowed freely through her like liquid sunshine. It was as if she were glowing from the inside out.

"No more kissin'. We gots to go," Josh interrupted them again.

Maddy pulled back as Turner wrapped his arm over her shoulders. "I think Josh is jealous. We may need to give him some more kisses, Mama."

"Nooooo." Josh shook his head and held up his action-figurine toy that Maddy had bought for him in the city with Jasmine. "You can kiss Black Panther instead."

Turner chuckled and picked Josh up, carrying him on his shoulders. "Alright, little man, I'll give you a break. But you should know I plan on kissing your mommy a whole lot."

Maddy caught Turner's wink. Butterflies tumbled in her belly. For once in her life, she was happy and safe. She wouldn't let someone with a grudge take this away from her. She would fight tooth and nail to reclaim what should have been hers.

Maddy had a feeling she was in for the fight of her life.

28

———————

MADDY

Maddy loaded the last of her groceries in the car and shut the trunk. She wiped the sweat from her brow. What a morning. After painting the shed, she'd rushed out to get the groceries, and now she couldn't wait to get out of the heat and into the air-conditioned car.

"Madeline?"

She turned. Hayley stepped out of an expensive-looking sports car with a familiar-looking man climbing from the driver's side.

"Small world, running into you again." Hayley smiled, her gaze roaming down Maddy's paint-stained shorts and sweaty muscle shirt.

Of all the times to run into her. "I guess it is."

"You remember my brother, Patrick?" Hayley motioned to the tall man beside her. He was handsome, with a clean-shaven sharp jaw and soft brown eyes. Images of a much younger, more gangly version of the man on her father's yacht flitted through her mind.

"I think so. How are you doing?" Maddy replied.

His eyes darted the length of her, but unlike his sister, he seemed to like what he saw. "Pretty good. You?"

"Oh, I know! We should totally have a double date sometime. She may not look like much now, but I know for a fact how Maddy can clean up." Hayley stuck her nose up and smiled as she delivered her backhanded compliment. "It will be just like old times. I'm sure Brett would love to see you."

Maddy's spine stiffened. "Who?"

Hayley's eyes gleamed like she'd won something. "Brett Holt. My fiancé. He was your date to prom, but I guess he eventually saw the light. I don't hold it against him." She laughed.

Just Brett's name sent a surge of violent sickness through her. Panic seized her lungs. Her senses switched to full alert as her mind spun. *Escape. Run away!* "I . . . I'm sorry. I have to go." Maddy numbly raced to the driver's side of the car, ignoring Hayley's huff before the clack of her heels faded.

Maddy started the car, putting the air conditioner on full blast as she sucked in a deep breath. Her skin itched and burned like a thousand fire ants were crawling on her. Flashes of that night, of Brett's grunts and the rancid alcohol on his breath, burst through her.

What do you see? Turner's voice cut through the fog.

Her eyes snapped open. *Trees, I see trees. I feel cold air. I hear my heart thudding in my ears.*

She licked her lips, though whether she tasted her sweat or her tears she wasn't sure.

She took long, deep breaths over several minutes until she was calm enough to drive home. She needed a cold shower and Turner's arms around her. He'd planned a date for them this evening. The last thing she wanted was to go out and be around people, but she didn't want to let him down. He would make her feel safe and grounded.

Two hours later, she'd kissed Josh goodnight, and said a quick thank-you to Gerry before Turner had opened his truck door and helped her inside. They were winding down the road further away from the center of town, where the properties grew farther and fewer in between.

"You gonna tell me where we're going now?" she asked.

He reached out and slid his fingers through hers on her lap. "We're almost to the first stop."

She tugged the red cocktail dress down her thigh nervously. She didn't like surprises. But she trusted Turner, which was something she never thought she'd say about another man.

"You look gorgeous tonight. Makes me want to skip all my plans and go straight to the part where I ravish you."

She giggled. "Ravish? Who even uses that word anymore?"

"I guess I do." He chuckled and put his blinker on, pulling into the driveway to a newer home with white siding and purple shutters. A motion-sensor light flicked on, illuminating the driveway.

"Where are we?"

He smiled and opened his door, releasing her hand to slide out before he shut her in and walked in front of the vehicle to her side.

She unbuckled while he pulled the handle and helped her from the vehicle. Her body pressed against his, her arms immediately seeking him out. Turner tucked her against his body, and they walked towards the house. She remained quiet as he led her to the front door where a lock with a keypad hung from the knob.

He pressed a few numbers and the box opened, revealing a key. Turner opened the door and led her inside. He flicked the light on, illuminating the small walk-in mudroom. It was empty, devoid of even a pair of shoes. She cast a questioning glance at him.

He winked and pulled her hand towards the next room, flicking the switch as he went. Next was a large kitchen with white cabinets and marble counters with an island in the center. The room was bare, empty. Was this house for sale?

"What are we doing here?" she asked again.

He pointed towards the next large room that was visible from the kitchen with the open-concept plan. "I figure we could get a big L-shaped couch to go there. We could put the TV over here."

She followed his finger and turned to him, her eyebrows drawing together. "We? Is this your house?"

Turner stepped closer, looking her in the eyes. "I was hoping it could be our house. A friend of mine is the real estate agent, and it's just about to go on the market. Places like this sell fast, so he gave me first dibs. It's got four bedrooms, two bathrooms, a big backyard that's perfect for Josh to run around in. There's even a stream back there. We can come with him in the daylight and check it out if you want. I believe the previous owners left the swings back there too."

Maddy swallowed and looked around in disbelief.

"If you don't like it, we can look at others." Turner's hand rested on her lower back.

She spun towards him. "It's gorgeous. But are you asking me to move in with you? Buy a house together?"

"I'm asking you for whatever you're willing to give. I want to build a life with you and Josh. And I know it will happen. I believe it. But I also know you may need some more time. If you tell me you could see yourself living here eventually with me, then I'm gonna buy it."

"You sound so sure that we . . . that this could be long term."

He cupped her face. "I'm not planning on going anywhere. I want you, Maddy. I've wanted you since before I knew what wanting truly was. But now it's turned into full-blown need. Like I'd only be half a man without you. Tell me I'm not in this alone. Tell me you feel it too."

Oh, God. Could she really believe it? Turner wanted to build a life with her? She swallowed, joy and disbelief bursting from her. She loved him too. She nodded. "I do. And it scares me."

"Never felt nothing as powerful as the love that I feel for you. I was so fucking angry when you came back into my life like a whirlwind." He chuckled. "You made me feel things I wasn't ready for. Scared me." He kissed one cheek and then the other before meeting her eyes again. "But I'm ready now. Ready to jump with you into the unknown, because I figure if I have you by my side, then I'll be flying, not falling."

Maddy's heart was about to burst through her chest. Turner's promises fell like shooting stars of wishes and hopes and dreams, all rolled into one magnificent explosion of pure love.

"Yes." She kissed him. His arms wrapped around her. A pleasant sound hummed in the back of his throat before he slipped his tongue into her mouth. She sucked, tasting him. He deepened the kiss, melding her lips with his, coaxing and teasing while his hands moved to grip her ass. He lifted her, and Maddy's legs instinctively wrapped around his waist before he set her on the island. The cold marble was a nice contrast to the heated arousal burning her skin.

Turner lifted her dress over her hips around her waist,

his mouth not leaving hers. She gripped the buttons of his shirt, undoing three before he pressed his wide hand to her chest, forcing her to lie back. Her chest heaved as she panted.

"You didn't wear any panties?" His voice grated, like he was barely hanging on.

She shook her head.

"Christ. Why not?" His chest expanded faster with each breath.

"I knew you'd appreciate the easy access."

"Fuck." His large, calloused hands kneaded the flesh of her ass. "I'm gonna make you come so hard, and you're gonna take it like a good girl, aren't you, princess?"

"Yes." Her voice left her in a pleading gasp. His dirty words turned the blaze in her core to an all-out wildfire of need.

The sound of his belt and the swoosh of his pants hitting the floor was the only warning before he pressed her thighs apart and pulled her so that her ass hung off the edge of the bench. He pulled a gold foil packet from his pocket.

Maddy held up her hand. "I'm clean and I get the shot. I want to feel all of you tonight."

Turner's eyes darkened, and he tossed the condom wrapper onto the counter. "I'm clean too. You sure?"

She nodded.

He thrust into her all at once, stretching her, filling her so completely. She surged up, wrapping her arms around his neck, her mouth dropping open as a scream left her lips.

Turner pressed his thumb to her clit, swirling and rubbing her into a frenzy as he slowly rocked back and forth inside her.

Pleasure spun within her, building a pressure that made her squirm.

"That's it, beautiful. Come apart. I've got you." Turner's

hips bucked harder and faster, matching the rhythm of his thumb.

Maddy leaned forward and kissed him, connecting with him in every way possible. "I'm going to—"

Her eyes widened as his blues locked on to hers. For one brief moment in time, nothing existed but their two souls crashing into one another. She shattered, her toes curling as a tidal wave of pleasure slammed into her, drowning her in a deluge of wanton bliss.

"So sexy. So perfect." Turner grunted, his face drawing into a serious and focused expression. His pupils were so large, like a gateway to another world. His hands dug into her hips, no doubt leaving bruises as he fucked her, bringing her higher and higher until another wave of her orgasm surged through her.

"Maddy!" he roared, his cock pulsing and emptying inside her.

She tensed around him, riding out the aftershocks of ecstasy as he held her in his arms. Nothing but the sound of their breathing echoed in the empty room. She leaned against him, her body boneless and limp. He held her up, his soft kisses tenderly roaming down her neck.

"Give me twenty minutes and we can do that again, only much slower this time." His hot breaths tickled her sensitive flesh.

When had she ever felt this happy? A warning niggled in the back of her mind—something was going to happen to bring her back to earth, to wake her from this dream and thrust her back into the nightmare her reality usually was. It was only a matter of time.

29

TURNER

Turner grabbed his wallet from the top of the dresser and slipped it into his pocket. His eyes scanned the bedroom until they landed on his phone, charging by the bed. He scooped it up, his attention falling on the new message alert. He tapped it.

Steph: *I will be in town this weekend with the paperwork. Want to go to Alfonso's in the city for memory's sake? I'd love to have a chance to talk before we sign.*

Turner breathed out a sigh of relief. This divorce process was almost over. Not that he disliked his soon-to-be ex-wife. She was a great friend. But that was all she was to him. They'd given it their best shot. Eventually they'd grown apart and fallen out of love. But now that Turner had been with Maddy, it made what he'd thought was love pale in comparison.

Turner: *Sounds good. Tell me what time to meet you there on Saturday.*

A soft rap on the door had him pocketing his phone as he looked up. A sliver of guilt weighed on his shoulders as Maddy gave him a warm smile.

"Hey, you."

He didn't see a reason to bring up the fact that he was legally a married man until after the papers were signed. With Maddy's past, it would only hurt her. Besides, his marriage had been over two years ago. They were just jumping through the legal hoops at this point. He'd wait until it was official and let her know that it was no big deal.

"Mornin', princess." Turner opened his arms and wrapped them around her. Maddy relaxed into him. God, she felt good.

She pulled away first, standing on her tiptoes to kiss his cheek.

"You wanna go out Saturday night? I have an errand to run around dinner, but after I get back, what do you say we go back to the house? I bet the code still works." He smiled. He'd light the whole room with candles and tell her everything.

"I have to work weekends. You know that."

His smile fell. "Right. I guess I didn't think you'd still work there with us moving in together."

"Well . . ." Her gaze darted to the side as if she were thinking.

"If you really want to continue dancing, I'll support you. I won't lie and tell you I like it. But if it truly makes you happy, I'll deal with it."

Her gaze volleyed back and forth between his eyes as if searching for an answer. "You'd support me taking off my clothes and dancing for other men?"

His jaw clenched and his hands balled into fists as unwanted images of her doing just that flicked through his mind. Jealousy reared its ugly head. "If it makes you happy." *Fuck, this is going to be one of the hardest things I've ever done.*

She kissed his lips, wrapping her arms around his neck before sliding her tongue in his mouth. He squeezed her tighter and groaned as she pulled away, leaving him trying to catch his breath.

"I don't actually love it. In fact, I hate it. But it was my only option to support Josh and—"

"And now, you have me," he interjected.

Her eyes grew glassy, disbelief and gratitude flashing in her watery gaze. "You mean that? You would love another man's child and take care of him, just like that?"

Turner pressed a kiss to her nose and then her cheeks. "He's a part of you. And he's just as lovable and maybe a tad cuter. It's the chubby cheeks. Sorry, princess, but it's true."

She chuckled. "He is pretty adorable."

He crushed his lips against hers, sliding his hands down her waist to grab handfuls of her ass.

"Mommy?" Josh called from down the hall.

She laughed as Turner gave her one more lingering kiss.

"In here, buddy," she answered, turning towards the door.

"I take it back. He loses points for being a cockblocker." Turner slapped her ass before she shot him a playful look over her shoulder.

"What's a cockblocker?" Josh asked as he turned the corner.

Turner blanched. Damn it, he really needed to start spelling things when Josh was home.

Maddy glared at him. "Yeah, Turner. What's a cock-blocker?"

"Uh, it's uh . . . a cock is a boy chicken and . . ." He looked pleadingly towards Maddy to rescue him.

She must have taken pity on him because she scooped up Josh in her arms, hiking him on her hip, and said, "Turner was using an adult word, honey. That's not one little boys should repeat. Okay?"

"Otay." Josh turned to him, giving him a look that made Turner doubt this would be the end of it.

"Let's go make dinner," Maddy suggested.

"Can we's have 'pegetti wis meatballs?" Josh asked, clapping his hands together like he was praying as he gave his mother pleading eyes.

"We don't have any ground beef. I used the last of it two days ago," Maddy answered.

"Uaaah." Josh's little chest deflated.

"I can run to the store. Spaghetti sounds good to me too. Need anything else?" Turner asked.

Josh perked up, his eyes sparkling as he licked his lips. Maddy and Josh spun to look at Turner. "Maybe some more parmesan too. You don't mind?" Maddy asked.

"Nah. I'll run out quick and be back before you know it." Turner pecked her lips on his way past.

"TT, no kissin' Mommy." Josh giggled.

"Are you jealous? Would you like one too? Maybe on your cheek?" Turner asked.

"No!" Josh snuggled against his mother and laughed.

"Alright. I guess I'll give this one I saved to your mommy." He peppered his lips across Maddy's cheek three times before he left them and jogged down the stairs.

The store was less than ten minutes away. He parked the truck and walked in, heading straight for the meat section, on a mission. He reached for the pound of ground beef.

"Well, well, look what the cat dragged in," a saccharine-sweet voice said behind him.

Turner gripped the cool package in his hands and turned around. Hayley stood there with her basket full of celery, cucumbers, and kale, with a package of Oreos peeking out from the bottom like she'd tried to hide them.

"Hayley." He nodded a polite greeting and moved to step past her, but she darted in front of him. "Can I help you with something?"

"Actually, I was wondering if maybe I could help you with something?" Her eyes raked over him suggestively before returning to his.

"Can't think of a single thing."

Her catlike gaze narrowed on him, turning calculating. She licked her lips before smiling "Really? It could be our little secret."

Okay, the time for politeness was over. "In the mood to slum it with the help? Isn't that what you said to Maddy?"

Hayley rolled her eyes. "Oh, come on now. We both know it would just be sex. It's not like a married man such as yourself could have more than a tryst, right?" She smiled like she'd won something.

A sliver of panic rippled through Turner. Would Hayley tell Maddy before he had a chance?

Turner leaned in with a smile, hoping to lull her into a false sense of hope. She bit, because she, too, angled closer conspiratorially. "You know the whole 'snobby mean girl' thing got old in high school. People like you will never be happy as long as you seek to use others for your own gain."

Hayley fumed, anger sparking in her eyes as her lips formed a straight line. "Don't even try to act like you're better than me, Turner. You're nothing but a gardener's son, just as you've always been and always will be."

He shrugged and backed up a few steps. "Better to be an honest, hardworking man's son than a vindictive bitch."

She gasped as he strode away with a satisfied smile on his

face. He wasn't going to let anyone ruin his good mood, especially a jealous trollop like Hayley. He needed to tell Maddy about Stephanie before she found out from someone else. Tonight, they'd have a nice dinner together, and then he'd tell her. Turner sighed. Surely, she'd understand. This situation was night and day to what had happened between Maddy and Josh's biological father. His marriage to Steph had been over for a long time. They'd been roommates for more than a year before divorce was even put on the table. And he was going to start a life with Maddy now. Turner had nothing to worry about. Right?

30

MADDY

Maddy tucked a strand of her blond hair behind her ear as she hummed to herself, stepping out into the cool summer evening. Turner and Josh were inside, watching an episode of *Paw Patrol* with Gerry. She needed to let her boss at The Pearl Necklace, Archer, know that she wouldn't be coming into work anymore.

She pulled out her phone and dialed. Her heart raced faster as it rang. Was she really ready to trust in a man again, and believe that he would be there to support her and Josh and work as a partner? She definitely wasn't ready for just any man, but this was Turner. And he'd promised to build a life with her and treat Josh as his own.

"The Pearl Necklace, Josie speaking."

"Hey, Josie, it's Scarlett. I'm calling in to give my notice to Archer."

"You're quitting?" Josie confirmed.

"Yes. Do I need to finish the two weeks out?"

Josie laughed. "This is a strip club, sweetheart, not Subway. You want to work two weeks or not, it's up to you."

"Not really."

"Have a nice life," Josie said before the line cut.

Maddy pulled the phone away from her ear and stared at it for a moment. Relief washed over her. Emotion welled in her eyes. She was done stripping to pay the bills. A smile split her face. The Pearl Necklace had been a great place to work. She'd felt safe there. Archer was the driving force behind the work culture there. He had strict rules and protected his employees. At least, that was what Maddy had seen. Maybe in the red room things were different? She'd never know now.

Maddy walked around the front of the house, the grass tickling her bare feet. Joy swelled in her chest as a freedom she had longed for enveloped her in a rush. She was so excited she didn't even watch where she was going. The moment her car came into view, she jumped back and gasped.

Red spray paint dripped from the doors like it was still fresh. The scent of chemicals made her stomach churn almost as much as the words. *Whore. Homewrecker. Liar. Slut.*

Maddy's gaze darted down the road. She backed up towards the front door. Birds sang in the trees, and the sun shone down—a complete contrast to the dark storm raging in her mind.

Why was someone targeting her? Why couldn't they just let her be?

"LEAVE ME ALONE!" she screamed, anger taking the place of fear. She looked over her shoulder. Those men couldn't terrorize her like this and expect no retaliation. She wouldn't let them have power over her again.

The door flung open. Turner ran outside, Gerry right behind him.

"What's wrong? Where—" Turner's voice halted, his face draining of blood as he stared at the words slashed across her car.

"What's wrong, Mommy?" Josh asked.

"Let's go inside and watch some more Chase and Skye, okay?" Gerry shut the door and led her son into the safety of his home.

Turner's arms wrapped around her, encompassing her in warmth and comfort. She leaned against him, holding on tight.

"I'm getting some cameras installed."

"Call the sheriff." She pulled away enough to look him in the eyes.

She lifted her chin and straightened her shoulders. "I'm done hiding in fear. I can't keep living like this. They want a fight? I'm not the same scared girl who was trapped in that limo with them. And I'm done letting men control my life because they feel entitled to take whatever they want from me. I'll tear their fucking faces off before I let them take one more thing from me."

Pride shone in Turner's eyes before he hugged her. "I'm so proud of you. And I'll be here by your side every step of the way."

"It's nice having someone in my corner." She gave him a small smile.

His gaze flicked back to the car and then to her. "You sure this couldn't be anyone else?"

Her brows drew together. "Like who?"

His eyes darted around. "Maybe someone from your past?"

"Scott, the man who broke into my apartment, was more straightforward. He wouldn't have the patience for this. This is calculating and purposeful. It was done by someone who's arrogant enough not to get caught."

Turner hesitated and then nodded. "Fits the Holts' description."

He pulled out his phone and pressed a button before bringing it to his ear. "Bently? Yeah, it's Turner. We have a problem . . . No, I didn't. It's nothing like that. Maddy's car was vandalized. Spray paint and looks like her tires are slashed."

Maddy turned back to her car, her shoulders sinking as she confirmed that her tires were in fact flat.

"Okay. See you soon." Turner hung up. "He'll be here in a few minutes."

A cold chill swept through her. Maddy crossed her arms over her chest as she shivered.

Turner slid his cell into his back pocket and wrapped her in his embrace once again. He kissed her forehead. "We'll get the bastards who did this, princess. I promise you and Josh will be safe with me."

She closed her eyes and slid her arms around his waist before laying her head on his chest. The steady thrum of his heartbeat gave her a sense of safety. "Thank you, Turner. You don't know how much this means to me. I've never had anyone I could count on. Not when it mattered." A small sob left her lips.

His big hand swept up her back, rubbing slow circles. "Sshhhhh. It's okay. I've got you, and I'm never letting go."

Her heart skipped a beat at his promise. Never in her life did she think she'd get to hear those words and believe them. But here she was. Her world was a mess as usual, the low after the high that always came—only this time, she wasn't alone. Maybe it was okay for her to let down her guard now that she had someone else to lean on.

31

———————

TURNER

Turner wiped the crumbs off the table and into his hand as Josh bounced up and down on his feet.

"I gets to drive the mower, Mommy!"

"I know, baby. But first you have to come brush your teeth and get dressed." Maddy held her hand out to him.

Josh ran around the room excitedly, ignoring her. "Then we gets ice cream."

Turner chuckled and dumped the crumbs from his hand into the garbage before rinsing the cloth. "We can't do either, bud, unless you listen to your mommy and get ready."

Josh made an airplane noise and zoomed past Maddy. She shook her head and sent Turner a smile. "I've never seen him so eager to do work before. Usually I have to trick him into thinking it's a game."

God, it was good to see some joy on her face after the nightmare of last evening's events. He'd wanted her to stay in his bed, but she wouldn't leave Josh. Woman was afraid that the monster in the shadows was going to come for her child. Turner didn't blame her. It tore him apart that he couldn't fix

175

this for Maddy. Those assholes were going to pay one way or another.

Turner focused on the little boy eagerly climbing up the last stair. He couldn't wait to take him for his first ride on the mower like his dad had done for him. "He's definitely a Walker boy now."

Maddy blinked, her eyes growing watery. Turner wiped his damp hands on his pants before cupping her face with them. "Hey, princess, what's wrong?"

She shook her head. "Nothing."

"Then why are you cryin'?"

She blinked, a tear sticking to her blond eyelashes. "Because you just keep getting better, and I can't believe you're mine."

He gently pressed his lips to hers before he pulled her in for a hug and nuzzled her neck. "I'm definitely yours, princess. And you're all mine." He squeezed the globes of her ass.

She giggled and swatted him away as she went up the stairs.

He smiled, his heart so full at the sight of her and the knowledge that she felt the same way about him as he did about her.

"I don't remember you ever looking so goo-goo-eyed over a girl in your life—even Stephanie." His father's voice drew his attention to the living room.

"Didn't know you were in here."

"Obviously." His father folded the newspaper and got up from the couch. "You taking today off?"

Turner nodded and leaned against the entrance to the kitchen. "Yeah, figured I'd do the yard here and then take them into town. Maybe head to the beach. I think they could both use a day to relax after yesterday."

His dad looked at him and sighed. "Yeah, they probably could. I'm glad you finally pulled your head out of your ass."

Turner chuckled. "Me too."

Both their attention darted to the front door as a knock sounded.

"Who could that be?" Gerry asked.

Turner pushed off the wall and walked to the door. He peeked out the small windows to the side of the foyer and froze. *Shit. What is she doing here?*

"Who is it?" Gerry asked, alert.

The knock sounded again.

Sweat beaded on his forehead as his mouth went as dry as the desert. He forced a swallow, his eyes wildly searching the space in front of him as if he'd find the answer there. Fuck! This wasn't how he wanted this to go down. But he had no choice.

Maybe he could get her out of here before Maddy came back downstairs. This wasn't how he wanted to tell her. He opened the door.

Steph smiled up at him brightly. "Hey, surprise. I got in town a day early. Thought I'd stop by and see your dad. I didn't expect you to be here too." She reached her arms out to hug him.

"Uh, yeah. I'm taking the day off."

She slid in beside him, entering the house before he could stop her.

"Maybe we should go outside and talk?" he asked.

"Oh, nonsense. I'm here to see Gerry." Steph gave his dad a big, genuine smile and a tight hug.

"Nice to see you, sweetheart," Gerry greeted her.

Turner cast a nervous glance up the stairs. Josh and Maddy would be down any minute.

"It's been too long since I've visited. I probably should

have come more when Turner was deployed. That's the thing with hindsight, as they say." Stephanie's gaze turned back to him and softened. "That's actually why I'm here."

Sweat trickled down Turner's temple as he tried to swallow the cotton ball lodged in his throat.

Gerry looked between them and cleared his throat. "I'll go get you a cup of coffee." He disappeared into the kitchen.

"Let's go out to the porch. It's a nice day." Turner started for the door, but Steph placed her hand on his arm halting him.

"I was hoping we could talk and maybe not sign those papers just yet. I think we should give our marriage another try. I know I wasn't good at communicating my needs, and we both got busy with our own lives. Maybe we could work back towards each other and find things we have in common again?"

What?

A thunk sounded upstairs. *Shit. Shit. Shit.*

"We can talk more over dinner tomorrow. How about that?" Turner asked, gently grabbing her arm to guide her outside.

He didn't even dare to check and see if his father overheard, afraid of what he would find on his dad's face.

"TT, who's that?" Josh's little voice asked from behind him.

Panic settled into Turner's gut like a boulder, his shoulders tensing as both he and Steph turned around to the little boy.

"Oh, you are adorable. I'm Stephanie, Turner's wife. Who are you?"

Turner cringed, his eyes darting towards the stairs where Maddy stood, her face pale and stricken. There was no doubt over whether or not she'd missed Steph's words.

"Maddy, I can explain." He stepped forward. Betrayal sparked in her eyes before they hardened like steel. He halted.

"You're married?" Maddy's voice trembled.

Turner moved forward, but his father gripped the back of his neck and squeezed firmly. "You didn't tell her?"

Maddy's attention darted to his father, betrayal shining in her blue orbs as she stumbled back a step before walking forward to scoop up Joshua. Turner didn't have to look in his father's disappointed eyes to know he'd fucked up big-time.

"It's not what you think, Maddy."

She didn't look at him, her face a hard, emotionless mask as she jogged up the stairs with her son on her hip. This couldn't be it. He just needed to explain. Surely Maddy would understand. *I should have told her last night.* But everything had been a mess then, and she'd been so shaken by the events with her car. *I have to make this right. I love her.*

"I'm sorry. I didn't realize." Steph's soft voice drifted over him.

He turned back to her. "I need to go, but we will have a conversation. I want to sign those papers tomorrow like we planned."

Stephanie and he had run their course. She was a good woman and a great friend, but that was all she ever would be. She was his past. His future was upstairs, and that was where he was headed.

32

MADDY

Maddy set Joshua on the bed, fighting the blur of tears that burned her eyes. Her body trembled with adrenaline as thoughts raced in her mind. *Turner is married. And Gerry knew.* How did she get here again? She had been betrayed, and now she had no one else to call. *I'm alone.* And Joshua was counting on her to not fall apart. Maddy didn't get that luxury. She may not have anyone, but Josh would always have her. How was it possible to be numb and have the most intense pain tearing her heart to shreds at the same time?

She picked up Josh's backpack with shaking hands. "Get your toys, buddy."

"Why, Mommy? Are we going to the park?"

She forced a smile, hoping to set him at ease. "We're gonna go on a trip."

"Is TT coming?" His little innocent face turned to hers, hopeful.

"Just us this time. Make sure you get every one." She handed him his backpack and hurried to grab her duffle bag, then stuffed their clothes inside it. The urge to run away crawled over her skin and sunk into her flesh.

"Maddy." Turner's voice was gruff and penitent as he stepped into the room.

Because he's been caught.

"TT, we're going on a trip," Josh supplied.

Maddy emptied the last drawer into the bag and hurried to zip it closed, but the damn zipper stuck. *Can't anything go right? Haven't I been put through enough?*

"Maddy, please let me explain." Turner reached out to her elbow, and she jerked it away.

"Don't you ever fucking touch me again." Her voice was cold and firm.

Turner's eyes widened as he held up his hands and backed away. Josh quieted, looking between them as if assessing the situation.

"Are you married?"

"Yes, but—"

"How could you?" She shook her head. "You knew about —" Maddy turned to Josh, her chest heaving.

Her son looked back at her, fear flashing in his eyes as he inched closer to his mother.

Maddy slung the bag over her shoulder and zipped up Joshua's backpack, then held it in her other hand as she picked up her son. Everything she needed was on her body. She spun towards Turner, chin up, ignoring the tears that slid down her cheeks and the regret hanging heavily between them.

"I told you I never wanted to be put in this position again —never wanted to be the other woman. You used me."

"No, we're separated and just waiting on the divorce paperwork. That's why she came—to sign the papers."

"You used me," she repeated, her voice cracking with emotion. "And what's worse, you promised no more secrets, no lies, and the whole time, you held this back. You had every opportunity to tell me."

"Princess, please. Let me explain." Tears welled in Turner's eyes, an ocean of sincerity swimming in them.

God, he was a good liar. She had no doubt he regretted not telling her, but was it because he got caught? It didn't matter, because he'd betrayed her trust for the last time. She would never believe him again. How dare he make her trust him, consider a future together, and keep something like this from her the whole time? He'd had every opportunity to say something.

Maddy pushed past him, shifting Josh's weight.

"Please, Maddy, don't go. I'll leave. Stay here." Turner gently grabbed her arm.

Maddy jerked away. Josh started to whimper, adding one more level of anxiety to the chaos spinning inside her.

"Maddy, please listen to Turner. Stay here where it's safe," Gerry's voice pressed from the top of the stairs. She turned towards him, one Walker on either side of her. A sliver of fear snaked down her spine. Never in a million years did she think either one of them would hurt her, but then again, they'd both lied to her. She didn't know them at all.

"And if I don't want to?" She flicked her gaze to Turner first.

His mouth parted as if realizing she was afraid of him. He backed up a step. "I love you, Maddy, but I'd never force you to do anything you didn't want to do. I won't give up on you either. I just want you and Josh to be safe."

She backed up, turning to Gerry. His eyes were watery too.

He lifted his palms up to halt her. "Please just take some time to calm down. You two need to talk and work this out. Don't run away."

She shook her head. "The only mistake I made was trusting you both and returning to this town. I should have never come back."

Maddy brushed past Gerry as Joshua's cries increased. "I want to stay with Papa and TT!"

Maddy clenched her jaw. She rushed out of the house. *Shit.* Her car was gone, towed away yesterday.

"Take my truck." Turner held out his keys.

She shook her head. "I don't need anything from you. I can take care of myself and my son on my own."

"Damn it, Maddy. Hate me, but don't do something stupid like put yourself at risk."

She whirled around. "I'm not your problem anymore. Go back to your house with your dad and your wife."

Turner's jaw clenched, those blue eyes flashing. Helplessness bowed his shoulders as he looked wildly towards the heavens like there was a magic rewind button up there.

Maddy turned and kept walking, hugging Joshua as the tears fell freely down her cheeks.

"Shhh, it will be okay, little prince. Mommy's here."

She walked until her arms screamed at her and her back ached. Until Josh's cries turned to whimpers and then to the soft steady breathing of sleep. She set the bags on the ground and moved Joshua's sweaty slumbering head higher on her shoulder as she dug out the phone from her pocket. Who could she call? She had no one.

Geo.

Maddy dialed her brother's number and held the phone to her ear.

"Hello? Mads?"

"Hey, Geo."

"Hey, what's up?"

"Are you in town still?" Maddy asked, her gaze wandering to the rising sun.

"No, the band and I are in California. We left last week."

"Oh, okay."

"Is everything alright?" Geo asked.

"No. It's not. But that's fine. I'll figure it out."

"If you need anything, Maddy, let me know. I can send you some money," Geo offered.

"I appreciate it. I'm okay on cash right now. I just need a place to crash until my car is fixed."

"I, uh, actually was staying at the house with Mom before I left. You should call her. Things have . . . she's different since Dad moved out."

"Dad moved out?" Maddy asked, stunned.

"I know she wanted to talk to you."

"Sure didn't seem it the way she ignored me a month ago," Maddy added sarcastically. Her brother had always gotten along better with their parents than she had. Not that their relationship was perfect by a long shot. But he wasn't the one they were ashamed of.

"Look, I know we aren't that close anymore. But you're my little sister, and I love you. I wouldn't tell you to do something unless I thought it could help. You can go there or I can rent you a room at The Lighthouse Inn."

Maddy shook her head. That was the first place Turner would look for her. She didn't want to see him again. Her heart had been damaged enough.

I won't give up on you.

His promise sent a rush of fresh heartbreak shattering inside her chest, like all that was left was broken glass.

She took a deep breath. "Okay. I'll reach out to her. And, Geo?"

"Yeah?"

"If Turner or anyone calls you asking about me, please don't tell them where I am, okay?"

"Did he do something? Do I need to get on a plane and kick someone's ass?" Geo's voice turned dark and deadly.

Maddy's eyes widened. He hadn't been the protective older brother since they were kids; they'd been too busy being enemies from junior high on. "No. Thank you though."

"Call me and let me know where you end up. I want to know you're safe," Geo said.

"I will."

"Talk to you later, sis. Tell my nephew I said hello."

"Okay. Bye, Geo."

"Bye, Mads."

She pulled the phone from her ear and dialed the number she knew by heart—the one she never thought she'd use again.

The voice that should send a rush of comfort through her answered; instead, it created a ball of anxious knots twisting in her guts.

"Mom? It's Maddy. I . . ." Could she risk being vulnerable again? Chance being rejected for the millionth time?

Maddy turned towards her son's sleeping face, his hair matted with sweat. Her heart squeezed. "I need your help."

33

MADDY

Maddy tucked Joshua into her old bed and placed a kiss on his forehead. She sat up and let her gaze wander over the room she grew up in. The posters of her favorite bands were still on the walls. Her dresser was filled with the sweet perfumes she used to wear. Everything was exactly how she'd left it the last night she'd been here.

Maddy focused on the spot on the floor in front of the bathroom. *Not everything.* The torn bloody dress was missing.

Maddy clamped her eyes closed, fighting the memories. She stood and left the room, keeping the door cracked open so she could hear Joshua if he woke. She wouldn't go far, but she needed some air.

"Madeline?" Her mother's voice halted her steps.

Maddy inhaled a fortifying breath and turned towards the frail but polished woman down the hall.

Maddy clasped her hands in front of her, straightening her posture out of habit. Her mother always had such a critical eye. *What does she think of me now?*

"Thank you for letting us stay here tonight. I'll call about my car tomorrow and see how much longer it will be until Josh and I can go."

Her mother's eyes shuttered closed before she swallowed and focused back on Maddy, motioning towards the small library on the second floor. "Can we talk?"

Maddy nodded, her stomach doing somersaults. She walked in, her mother following. They took seats across from each other in the padded cream-colored overstuffed chairs. Maddy rarely went into this room growing up here. Each wall was covered in books; there was even one of those ladders on rails that allowed it to move around the shelves. Then she hadn't been interested in books. Now, she saw the room for the treasure it was.

"I'm glad you called." Her mother's voice brought Maddy's attention back to the woman she never thought she'd see again.

"Oh?"

"After you came here working on the yard, I thought I'd hallucinated. I was so consumed with guilt for just walking away from you like that. I told myself for years if I ever saw you again, I would do what I could to help you . . . and then when it happened, I failed, just like always."

Maddy studied her mother closer. What was she saying?

Her mother tucked her hands into her lap like the prim and proper lady she was. "I was too ashamed to come to you. And as I sat across from your father at dinner and stared at my glass of wine, I . . . got so angry. I told him that I ran into you. Told him I wanted to make things right and he . . . well, you know your father. He didn't agree."

Didn't agree was likely the understatement of the century. Her father probably threw the dinner at the wall and screamed until his face turned beet red.

Her mother continued, her gaze meeting Maddy's. "I filed for divorce the next day, and I started going to AA meetings. It's been one month since I've had a drink. And I know it doesn't begin to make up for what I let happen to you, but I'd like to help you in any way you need. You and Joshua are welcome to stay here as long as you want. I understand I have no right to ask this, but I'd love to get to know him."

Maddy sat there, stunned. How was this happening? How was this real?

"Please say something." Her mother's voice came out in a whisper.

"I don't know what to say. I never thought we'd have this conversation. I didn't believe you'd ever . . ."

"I'm so sorry for that. I should have been there to protect you when you needed me."

More tears welled in Maddy's eyes. The impact of her mother's apology loosened something within her. Never in a million years had she expected this.

Maddy met her gaze. "As a daughter, your words mean a lot to me. As a mother, I can't imagine doing the things you did or letting them happen."

Her mother nodded, her shoulders lowering as her head bowed as if decades of guilt weighed on her.

"I don't think we'll ever get to the point where we can have a mother-daughter relationship," Maddy confessed.

"I understand."

"This is a lot. I just need some time to digest this. Figure out what I'm comfortable with," Maddy added.

"Of course. I'll be here when you're ready. I'll leave you to rest." Her mother stood and headed for the door.

"Mom?"

Her mother stopped and turned towards her, emotion

welling in her eyes. Maddy had never seen her mother cry. Susan Miller was never anything but put together and perfect.

"Thank you."

She nodded and disappeared out into the hall.

Maddy relaxed into the seat, hugging her knees against her chest. So much had happened in the last few hours. This morning, she'd been happy and safe. She'd been going to move in with Turner and give Joshua the family she'd always hoped for. And then everything had come crashing down.

Whether Turner was a signature away from divorce or not, the fact that he'd kept it from her was such a huge betrayal considering everything she'd shared with him about Josh's biological father. After those photos, he'd promised not to keep anything from her like that again.

Gerry's face flashed in her mind. A fresh blast of hurt brought fresh tears to her eyes. Gerry had known the whole time and never said anything. *So much for being like a daughter to him.*

And now she was back at her parents' home, a place she'd never thought she'd return to. Everything had come full circle. Maddy was alone. Someone was after her. What she thought she knew was a lie. Everything was spinning out of control and she had no one to lean on. She was drowning.

Why can't you just listen?

Smile.

Be polite.

Don't fuss.

It's just boys being boys.

You were asking for it.

It's your fault.

Good-for-nothing little slut.

Righteous anger swelled in her chest, igniting a fire inside her. She shook her head.

"I'm enough," she said aloud, more confident than she felt.

She'd survived so much in her twenty-six years—assault, an unexpected pregnancy, being a single mom—and she'd survive this too. Because that was who she was—a survivor.

She'd do whatever she had to in order to keep her little boy safe and live her life out of the shadows. She was done being ashamed. Done hiding. Done relying on men who promised to protect her and then wielded the sword that pierced her heart.

"Never again," she promised herself.

It was time to take control of her life. It was time she spoke her truth, no matter who believed her.

People could say what they wanted about her, but she was finished being the quiet, polite, obedient girl they all knew. Now they could deal with the woman who didn't give a fuck. It was time she did something she'd been too scared to do before. It was time Maddy went on the offensive.

34

TURNER

One week later, Turner opened the certified envelope that had been overnighted to him and scanned the pages. He was officially divorced. Setting the paper on his bed, he scrubbed a hand through his hair. He'd searched for Maddy and Joshua at every hotel and motel in town and in the cities surrounding Shattered Cove. Was she still here? Was she safe? Had whoever was after Maddy, gotten to her?

"How could I be so stupid?" He clenched his fists on his knees.

Picking up his phone, Turner scanned the text messages he'd sent. Maddy hadn't responded to a single one, nor his voicemails. No one had seen her or Josh. He'd even gone by the club. None of the employees would give him any information about Maddy, or Scarlett, as they knew her there. He'd gone to The Pearl Necklace after dinner with Stephanie, but Maddy had never showed.

Stephanie and he had parted on good terms. Explaining he'd fallen in love with someone else hadn't been fun. But

Steph had wished him well. He hoped she found her happiness, too, someday. Every second that ticked by was an eternity. Some psycho was after Maddy and he'd fucked up his chance to protect her. He'd ruined any chance she'd trust him now. Could she still love him?

Turner's phone chirped. He slid to the new message.

Jasmine: *Maddy messaged me and told me she and Josh are safe.*

Turner hit call.

"Yes?" Jasmine answered. The sound of several voices mumbled in the background like she was in a crowd.

"She messaged you? What else did she say?"

Jasmine sighed. "I don't know where she and Josh are staying. But they're safe."

"I need to talk to her."

"Turner, were you really still married to Steph the whole time?"

He let out a frustrated grunt. "We've been legally separated for over a year. Our marriage was over long before that. We were just waiting on the paperwork. We agreed to go our separate ways and see other people. I didn't cheat on my wife."

"But you didn't think to tell the woman you were dating?" Jasmine spoke slowly as if he were a child.

"I fucked up. She was already dealing with so much. We didn't exactly start out on the best of terms. When she told me about Josh's dad, I didn't even . . . It's not the same thing. At least, I didn't think it was. Then we argued over something else I did, and I didn't want to rock the boat. I was planning to tell her Saturday night after the papers were signed."

"I guess that didn't work out the way you planned. But can you blame her?" Jasmine mused as voices rose in the background.

"I can't. But, fuck, Jaz. How do I fix this?"

"I'm not sure you can, Turner. Everyone in Maddy's life has let her down or broken her trust. When Atlas walked away from me, I thought it was truly over between us." Jasmine took a deep breath, letting it out before she continued. "It took a long time for him to earn back my trust. He had to prove to me he wouldn't run again. And, in your case, I think Maddy needs to know you won't lie to her again— that you'll support her without you trying to control the situation with your misguided sense of protection. She's not a child who needs you to hide the realities of the world from her. She's a woman who needs a partner to stand by her side."

Turner nodded. "You're right. I need to find her so I can do that though."

Jasmine was quiet a moment before she spoke. "Turn on *Channel Six News*."

His brows drew together. "What? Why?"

"Just do it." Cheers erupted on the other end of the phone before Jasmine ended the call.

Turner stared at his phone a moment before he stood and raced downstairs to the living room. He grabbed the remote from beside his father and switched the channel.

"What are you doing?" his dad protested. "The game is on."

"Just hold on." He switched on the news.

A crowd had gathered around some men at a podium in front of city hall. Brett and Chris Holt were there as well as Hayley and a few others including Timothy Miller, Maddy's dad, and Brett Holt's father, the CFO of Holt Enterprises.

Turner's shoulders tensed as the cameraman zoomed in at Chris stepping up to the microphone.

"Hello, good people of Shattered Cove and New Hampshire. For those of you who don't know, I'm Chris Holt of

Holt Enterprises. I am honored to be a part of this city and am here to announce my candidacy for city councilman."

Cheers from the crowd rose as Turner's stomach hardened and his veins burned with anger. Why would Jasmine want him to see this? What was she trying to tell him?

Wait—was she there? It had sounded like she was in a crowd.

He sat on the edge of the couch, leaning towards the TV.

"You that interested in politics?" his dad asked.

Turner shook his head. "Those are the men who hurt Maddy."

Gerry's chair creaked as he, too, leaned forward. "Son of a bitch."

"Do you see Jasmine in the crowd?"

After a beat, Gerry responded, "No."

While Chris droned on, the camera switched between him and the crowd. Two bodies moved in a shuffle before the woman he'd searched for during the past week appeared.

Relief mixed with apprehension swirled inside him, tangling Turner's insides. What was she doing on stage approaching the Holts?

Part of him wanted to run out the door and race to city hall to save her. The other didn't want to miss a moment of this. Jasmine had told him to watch, not meet her. She must have had a reason.

Maddy needs to see that you'll support her without trying to control the situation with your misguided sense of protection. She's not a child who needs you to hide the realities of the world from her. She's a woman who needs a partner to stand by her side.

Jasmine's words echoed in his mind. Turner remained on the couch, his gaze riveted on the television.

It was time he did this Maddy's way.

35

MADDY

Maddy sucked in a heavy breath, her lungs turning to iron. The crowd cheered around her as nerves pricked her skin like a thousand tiny needles, her throat constricting. Bile churned in her gut, working its way up her throat at the sight of the two men who'd taken so much from her, and her own father who stood proudly beside them. Their fake smiles and bleached teeth taunted her.

Dirty slut. You wanted this.

Maddy clamped her eyes closed as dizziness spun in her head, the crowd getting louder as Chris's voice droned on about what he would do for the city.

A firm, warm hand enveloped hers and squeezed. Maddy opened her eyes and turned to the fearless woman by her side.

Jasmine leaned closer. "We don't have to do this if it's too much. I'm here for you either way."

Maddy turned back to the stage, the physical embodiment of her trauma, and then to the crowd of people buying his sugar-laced lies. Her gaze drifted towards the women in the audience. There was no way the Holts' offenses had ended with her. Sometimes it took one person standing up and saying something to instigate change. *I might not get justice, but they need to know what a monster he is.*

Maddy turned back to Jasmine. "I won't keep their dirty secret anymore. I have nothing to be ashamed of. It's time they face the repercussions of what they did."

Jasmine gave her a nod, and with a determined look in her eyes, she squeezed her hand again. "Let's do this, then."

Maddy's heart raced, her skin flashing hot and cold as she took the first step towards the stage. Maddy walked in front of the dozens of newscasters, Jasmine at her side. Time slowed. The doubts in her mind were drowned out by the blaring screaming of a young girl whose voice needed to be heard. She was only two feet from the men who had torn her life apart. Dark empty eyes full of anger turned towards her. They widened just a fraction before she focused on the crowd of questioning faces, years of pain and anger surging in her chest.

"Chris and his cousin, Brett Holt, are rapists."

Silence descended over the crowd. Cameras swiveled in her direction. The people were listening. It was now or never.

"Security!" Chris demanded.

Maddy swallowed down the lump in her throat, the invisible hands of society and shame squeezing and trying to silence her. "I was eighteen when they held me captive in a limo on my high school prom night. They forced me. They assaulted me. And they told me that if I wanted to live, I had to do what they said."

A shrill scream came from Hayley before she lifted her hand to her head and fainted. Brett didn't even bother checking on her; a security guard knelt by her side. Maddy rolled her eyes.

Murmurs and a few gasps came from the people gathered around the stage.

"What is your name?" one of the female reporters asked.

"Madeline Miller."

"She's a stripper," Chris argued, turning to Maddy's father. "I'm sorry, Timothy. I know this is embarrassing for you. You see, folks, Miss Miller is a troubled woman. She ran away from home and fell into a life of dubious choices and career. This is just a ploy for money and attention."

"Yes. I was an exotic dancer. But being a sex worker doesn't make me any less valid. What you and your cousin did to me was rape. And now everyone will know what monsters you really are."

A few beefy security guards moved in but the uniformed officers stepped up and spoke to them as planned.

She faced Chris, her chin held high. "You told me no one would believe me because of my occupation and because I was just one woman. So, I ask, how many of us will it take?" Maddy turned back towards the crowd. "How many women must one man hurt, cause irreparable trauma to in order for you to take us seriously?"

"Well, Miss Miller, there is only one at this point." Chris gave a laugh. His neck was tinged with redness—it was the only outward sign that this scene was bothering him.

"We both know that isn't true. I'm far from alone!" Maddy yelled.

Jasmine stepped forward. "They both tried to drug me."

"They assaulted me." A smaller voice from a woman on the other side of the stage inched forward.

"Lies!" Chris denied it angrily.

"Me too." Another woman stepped forward, her voice shaking as she took the first woman's hand. A line formed behind her as more and more women joined in until sweat broke out on Chris's forehead. He turned towards Brett and then to Maddy. Rage flashed on his expression.

Maddy drank in the faces around her who seemed stunned by the multiple women who stood before them, all echoing the same sentence. *"Me, too."*

Maddy raised her voice, her determination and confidence rising, too, as she stood with her sisters. Women she didn't know, but who all shared the same horrific past. "How many women's bodies must be violated, her words doubted, her reputation dragged through the mud before you believe us?"

Chris huffed and stepped closer to the microphone. "Enough! This is ridiculous. They are just trying to smear my name—"

"I'm not weak. My value is not based on what I do. But there is power in numbers, so here we are. Women you violated, drugged, raped, coerced, and we're standing together to say, 'No more.'" Maddy's head spun. The more she spoke, the more powerful her voice became. She looked Chris in the eyes and then turned to his cousin. She smiled confidently. "Just imagine how many women will come forward now that this is on TV. And your father's friends in government won't be able to impede the investigations into the evidence that's been sitting on shelves for years. That DNA will be matched and you will pay for your crimes."

"What are you talking about, Miss Miller?" a newscaster to her right asked. "How far up does this go?"

"You bitch!" Brett surged forward, his face red with an angry vein popping in his forehead.

Maddy stepped back as Bently moved forward, grabbing

Brett before he could touch her and forcing him onto the ground of the stage.

Bently handcuffed him. "Brett Holt, you're under arrest for the rape of—"

"This is all a misunderstanding. My cousin's actions have no reflection on me," Chris argued, throwing Brett under the bus just as Maddy and Bently had hoped.

"You bastard! You were there. You fucking gave me the pills," Brett yelled as Bently pulled him off the floor.

Another uniformed figure stepped forward holding up a pair of cuffs. She might not have been able to do this without the Shattered Cove Police Department's help. When Jasmine had convinced her to go to Bently, Maddy was surprised that he'd been more than happy to help. She wasn't sure how, but he'd found more than half the women standing up to speak out against the Holts. He'd advised her to wait until they had the warrants to say anything, and she'd asked him to wait to make the arrests until she'd had her say on the Holts' very public stage.

Deputy Vargas tipped her head to the side, her eyes narrowing in disgust at Chris. "Turn around and put your hands on your head."

"There is a misunderstanding. You have no evidence." Chris struggled.

"Should I add 'resisting arrest' to your charges?" Vargas quipped.

"Just go. We'll figure this out. Don't say anything without a lawyer," Brett's uncle stepped forward.

Chris turned around, his hands on his head as he speared Maddy with a threatening look. "This isn't over."

A shiver ran through Maddy, but she held her ground as Vargas read Chris his rights.

"What the hell do you think you're doing?"

It was the first time her father had spoken to her in eight years. Venom poisoned his tone, as his chest heaved.

Maddy crossed her arms over her chest and leveled her gaze on the man who was supposed to love and protect her. "I'm doing what I should have done long ago. I'm standing up for the young girl with the bloody, ripped dress who came to your office and told you what those men did to her. I'm doing what you should have done eight years ago. I'm taking my power back."

Maddy spun on her heel and climbed off the stage with Jasmine beside her. Camera flashes blinded her as newscasters surrounded them, blasting questions at them and the dozen women at their side. Maddy turned to her left. Pride and determination shone from the women's eyes. Brett and Chris might not get the time in jail that they deserved—rapists hardly ever did. The statistics proved it. Out of one thousand rapes, less than four hundred were ever reported, and out of that, only six resulted in jail time. These men had friends in high places and money to back them, making them even less likely to do time. But maybe because of the number of victims something would be done.

Maddy didn't regret speaking out because standing up to them loosened something inside her, setting it free. And it had given these other women the same opportunity to feel what she was feeling too.

She had worked diligently with Bently, Vargas, and Jasmine to ask old high school friends and their other connections. They'd found more people harmed by these two men than those who'd appeared here today. Some had decided they wanted no part in bringing up the past or having to show their face publicly. Maddy understood, and cast no blame on them. This was a personal decision that each survivor needed to make based on what was best for them. But she'd needed to speak up and put a stop to the harassment and a life lived in fear.

Her life might not have been perfect, and her heart may have been broken, but at least she could reclaim some of her power. *I'm choosing me from here on out.*

36

MADDY

addy sat at the table, drinking the cup of coffee her mother's maid had prepared. She opened the news app on her phone and scanned the latest article about the previous day's events.

Chris and Brett Holt have been charged with multiple counts of sexual assault and other charges relating to the use of Rohypnol on their alleged victims. Though the original charges had only eleven victims' names, more have since come forward. The Shattered Cove Police Department asks that anyone with information on this case come forward and contact them immediately.

"Mommy, look what Grandma got me." Josh held up a truck with a remote controller.

Maddy smiled. "That's so cool."

"Black Panther can drive it too!" He shoved the action figure in the open window of the vehicle. "Come on, Grandma. Me take it outside."

"Okay, sweetheart. Let me talk to your mom for a minute and then we'll go." Her mom smiled at him and then turned to Maddy, lowering her voice. "It's your brother's old truck from storage."

"I can't believe that thing still works." Maddy took another sip of her coffee as her gaze wandered as her son played by her mother's feet, something that seemed surreal.

"I saw the news. I won't ask why you didn't bother to tell me what you were going to do. But I wanted to let you know I'm proud of you." Her mother's voice wavered, tears shining in her eyes.

Maddy nodded. "Thanks."

"I, uh, didn't know if I should tell you, but I did keep the dress."

Maddy stood, her eyes widening. "My prom dress?"

Her mother nodded solemnly. "I sealed it in a bag and kept it in a safe. I don't know why I did it. Your father told me to destroy it, but I couldn't."

Maddy's chest squeezed. In some small way, her mother had defied her father for Maddy. But it was too late.

"The statute of limitation has passed for me since I was eighteen at the time of assault. But it means a lot that you did that." Maddy's shoulders lowered as she breathed out a sigh. *If I had come back two years ago, maybe . . . It doesn't matter. What's done is done.*

"Can we go now?" Josh asked before making car engine revving noises.

"Of course. I guess we're going to the backyard. Would you like to join us?" her mother asked.

Maddy shook her head. "Actually, I have some calls to make, if that's okay?"

Her mother smiled. Maddy hadn't left her alone with Joshua unless she was in the next room before now. "Of course. I'll have Sierra bring us out some snacks."

Maddy waited for Josh and her mother to walk out before she picked her phone back up, clicking on the voice message from Turner from the previous night. The time stamp was from right after she'd made her speech. No doubt Turner had seen it. Was she ready to hear his voice?

The fact was, he'd broken her trust. How could she believe he was genuine? That he truly loved her if he kept important things from her?

She lifted the phone to her ear. Turner's voice was rough and raw, sending an ache to her chest.

"Maddy, princess, I just watched you on TV. I'm so fucking proud of you. I wish I could have been there to see those pricks' faces in real life when you cut off their balls and fed them to them . . . I want you to know I get it. I understand what I did hurt you. I'm so fucking sorry . . ." He sighed, then silence permeated the message. "I know I have no right to ask you this, but I would never forgive myself if I didn't try at least one more time to speak with you. I love you, princess. And if you need me to let you go, I will. But I need to hear you say it to my face. Because I'm not ready to stop fighting for us. You own me, heart and soul, and—"

The voicemail ended. Maddy pulled the phone from her ear and scanned for another message, but there wasn't one. Disappointment flooded her.

Turner's words repeated in her mind. What did she want? Did she truly want to go her own way? Could she trust Turner enough to give him another chance?

Maddy walked out of the sitting room towards the grand staircase, making her way to her room. She sat on the bed, staring at the side table. She reached out, pulling the drawer open. A worn, makeshift paper passport sat on top of a pile of pictures. Maddy pulled it out, memories rushing over her.

"Hey, princess. Look what I found." An eighteen-year-old version of Turner handed over the rectangle paper booklet.

Maddy's eyes scanned the item. Maddy's Passport *was written on top in Turner's blocky, masculine script. Her brows drew together as she leaned against the outside building of the school and flipped the first page open. The first destination was the Bahamas.*

"I figured you'd want somewhere warm and tropical for the first visit. I can see you now with a bikini and coconut drink with those little umbrellas in your hand." Turner smiled and laughed.

Maddy's heart raced and her chest felt like someone had put it into a vise. This was the most precious gift anyone had ever given to her. Turner had listened that day on the bleachers.

He flipped the page and pointed to the tiny fortune cookie. "And the next is China. The food there has to be off the chain."

Maddy giggled. "You do know that fortune cookies are a Western invention and not from actual China, right?"

Turner frowned. "Oh."

Guilt crashed through Maddy. "Turner?"

"Hmmm?" Turner kicked the wall absentmindedly as he stuck his hands into his pockets.

"This is by far the best gift I've ever received."

His eyes lit up, but his brows arched skeptically. "I doubt a few scribbles on paper can beat a BMW for your sixteenth birthday."

She stepped closer, his breathing hitched as those blue pools dropped to her lips and then returned to her eyes. "I guess coming from money has shown me that the important things can't be bought."

"Maddy, I—"

"Walker! Let's go, man. We're gonna miss the team bus," one of the guys on the team interrupted, breaking their moment.

"I'll see you later, princess." He leaned in like he was going to kiss her and then backed away, giving her a wink. Butterflies burst in her belly.

Maddy's eyes darted to the door. The sound of footsteps drew her out of the memory.

She shoved the booklet back into the drawer and stood as the last person she expected to see walked into the room.

"What are you doing here?"

37

MADDY

"What are you doing here?" Maddy asked.

Hayley leaned against the doorframe, her purse hanging from her elbow. Her long skirt billowed around her knees. "This place hasn't changed since high school."

Maddy straightened her shoulders, a niggle in the back of her mind setting off alarms. "How did you know I was here?"

Hayley shrugged. "Not many other places you could be. Plus, your dad mentioned what happened between Susan and him. I put two and two together."

"What do you want, Hayley?" Was she mad about finding out her fiancé was a monster?

Hayley laughed and walked in, closing the door behind her. "What do I want?" she repeated, shaking her head as her laugher rose. "You made quite the spectacle of yourself yesterday. I thought, after everything, you'd learned your lesson."

Maddy stepped back, confusion swirling inside her. "What do you mean, after everything?"

"But you always did seem too stubborn and stupid for

your own good," Hayley replied ignoring Maddy's questions. Her eyes narrowed as she opened her purse and stuck her hand in. "You ruined everything. After prom, you were supposed to come back to school where I'd let the rumors fly, leak the recording of that night. But you ran away instead."

The blood drained from Maddy's face. "You knew about the recording?"

Hayley's mouth curved in a depraved smile. "Do you know how good it felt to hear you beg them to let you go? To listen to you promise to do whatever they said?"

Flames blistered Maddy's flesh as she staggered back. Hayley had seen the video of that night? She'd known the whole time?

"Why?"

Hayley's lips thinned as she narrowed her eyes once again. "Because everyone chose you. Madeline Miller, most popular girl in school, prom queen. You had everything that was supposed to be mine!"

Maddy swallowed, shaking her head. "You're mad at me because I was popular?"

"Even my own father chose you!" Hayley screamed.

"Dale?"

"No, you ignorant little baboon. My biological father, Timothy Miller." Hayley scowled.

The meaning of Hayley's words crashed over Maddy. "We're half sisters?"

"You never wondered? Are you that dense?" Hayley scoffed.

Maddy's spine stiffened as she snapped, "I was a pretty self-absorbed person in high school. Trust me, you didn't miss out on anything. The man is an asshole."

"When you came back, I thought maybe this was another chance. Maybe I could finally ruin you. Instead, you fucked everything up." Hayley's purse dropped to the floor as a shiny knife glinted in the rays of the sun seeping from Maddy's bedroom window.

Maddy's eyes widened. She held up one hand and reached for her phone with the other. "Hayley——"

"Don't even think about it." Hayley lifted the knife, stepping closer. Maddy backed up until the back of her knees hit the bed.

"Hayley, please, let's talk about this."

"You took everything I ever wanted. Every boy in school only had eyes for you. I had to make you dirty and unwanted. It was the only way. Then everyone would see how I was the one who deserved it all." Hayley's voice had turned hysterical, her eyes wild as she waved the knife in the air.

Was Josh safe? How do I get out of this? Hayley was blocking the only exit.

"But no, you came back to town and picked right back up where you left off. You and that gardener. Even the help wanted you."

Maddy froze. "It was you. The pictures. The car. You've been following me."

A glazed look shone in Hayley's gaze. "She finally gets it when it's too late. You are done taking things from me. And you're going to pay for ruining my life." Hayley lunged at her.

Maddy lifted her arms to block her attacker, screaming. The knife slashed, and a burn ripped through her cheek before searing pain erupted in her side. Blood leaked from the wound on her face. She sucked in a breath, a million needles of throbbing pain erupting in her side with the movement. She looked down, examining the weapon sticking out from her body. Her vision going hazy. No, this couldn't be the end. Josh needed her. Maddy was all he had. *I have to fight!*

38

TURNER

Turner walked up the steps to Maddy's parents' house. This was the last place he thought she'd be, but it was the only one left for him to check. He rang the doorbell and straightened his shoulders. He just needed to find her. He'd leave her be if that was what she truly wanted, but he wanted to see her face one more time and tell her everything he'd held back.

The door opened and a tall woman with an apron answered. "Hello?"

"Hey, I'm wondering if Maddy—uh, Madeline Miller is home?"

"Are you a—"

A scream interrupted the woman. Turner pushed past her and raced up the stairs. He'd know that voice anywhere. His heart pounded and his senses sharpened as he ran. A *thunk* from the closed door to his left had him ripping the door open.

His eyes were immediately drawn to the two figures in the center of a bedroom. Maddy's fist landed on the woman lying prone underneath her before she looked up. Her face was bloody and her blond hair, messy. Her other hand held a knife.

"Maddy!" Turner ran to her, scooped her up and carried her to the doorway, his gaze flicking to the woman on the floor and then raking over Maddy as he set her on her feet.

"Turner," Maddy gasped.

"What happened? Are you okay?" He ran his hands over her.

Maddy's legs gave out and she winced. Turner wrapped his arms around her, supporting her. His eyes went to her hand pressing into her side as blood oozed between her fingers. "Fuck, you're hurt."

"Mommy!" Josh and Susan Miller came running up the stairs.

"Stop," Turner commanded. "Call the cops. Get him out of here."

"I want Mommy!" Josh's cries rose as Susan warily picked him up and came closer.

"What's going on? Madeline?" Her mother's face blanched as her eyes landed on her daughter.

"Go, Mom, get Josh out of here! Do what Turner said." Maddy winced as if talking hurt.

Her mother hesitated one more moment, like she was torn between helping her daughter and getting her grandson away from this disaster. Finally, she spun around and raced downstairs.

Turner swiveled back to Hayley who started laughing as she rose to her feet. Her eye was swollen and her nose bloody.

"Let's go. The police will handle her." Turner wrapped his arm around Maddy, about to pick her up, when a glint of metal caught his eye.

"Not so fast. She's not going anywhere." Hayley pulled the gun from her thigh under her dress.

Turner didn't think; he acted. He dropped his hold on Maddy, charging the gun as Hayley fired. Pain bloomed in his chest as he took the bullet meant for his love, but he didn't stop. He dove, tackling Hayley to the ground. His hand gripped the weapon. The bitch wouldn't let it go. He twisted it from her hand, pointing it at her as he crawled backwards to the door and a slumped Maddy.

His chest screamed at him. Each breath was filled with shards of glass. The metallic taste of blood tainted his mouth.

Hayley heaved out a breath as sirens blared outside. Tears fell down her cheeks. She stood, wavering before turning to the open window.

Hayley turned to Maddy. "You did this." She didn't hesitate before she jumped out the window. A sickening *thud* sounded a moment later.

Susan shouted somewhere in the distance but it was muffled.

"She jumped out the window," Maddy yelled to the men in uniforms who entered the room guns drawn. "We need an ambulance up here now!"

Maddy's arms wrapped around him as the room darkened.

"Turner, hold on, okay? They're coming. Help is on the way."

"I love you, princess."

"I know. I love you too."

"Coming here . . ." He sucked in a breath, but his lungs didn't feel right. They hurt, and his chest was heavy. This was it. He lifted his bloody hand and dragged his knuckle across her cheek. "To tell you I'm sorry."

Tears tracked down her face. "I know. Shhh, don't talk about that now."

His breathing grew ragged. He coughed, red speckles flying onto her fair skin. The pain in his chest ebbed until he couldn't feel anything at all. Figures surrounded him—a medical team, shouting orders and asking questions.

Maddy clung to him. "Stay with me, Turner. Don't go. Fight. Please. I love you. Don't go. I need you."

Love you too, princess. He tried to say the words out loud but he couldn't get the air to speak.

Blackness engulfed him until all that was left was memory after memory of her smiling face. If only he'd told her the truth from the beginning. If only he'd not fucked up.

If only he had more time.

EPILOGUE - MADDY
THREE MONTHS LATER

Maddy set the bouquet of flowers on the stone grave. She tucked her coat closer, protecting herself against the chilly fall wind. She stood and walked away. She hadn't been ready, but after three months, it was time to put her past behind her for good. She couldn't go back and change it. The only thing she could do was take the lessons she'd learned and surround herself with people who were honest and truly cared for her.

Maddy made her way to her car, driving home in silence. She parked in front of the house that she and Turner had looked at together so long ago. The memories of their night here flooded over her. It seemed like it had taken place in another lifetime.

She walked to the door, going inside to the warmth of their home. Josh ran up to her. "Mommy, you're here!"

"Hey, sweetie. Did you have a good day with Papa Walker?" She hugged him and hung up her coat before toeing off her boots.

"Yep. We played all day and read lots of books." Josh's eyes lit up.

Maddy threaded her fingers through his hair and brushed it back. "Sounds like you had fun."

"I told him he could spend the night if that's okay with you?" Gerry asked, walking into the room. Maddy smiled at him. It made her feel better to know that things were good between the two of them again.

"My bag is already packed." Josh puffed his chest out proudly.

"I guess you're all set, then." Maddy kneeled to give him one more big kiss and hug.

"Bye, Mommy." Josh waved, running past her to get his shoes on.

Gerry grabbed his coat from the rack and slid his arms inside it. "Have a good night. I'll see you tomorrow."

Maddy waved as they left and she locked the door behind them. She walked through the house, admiring the cozy decor that she'd picked out herself.

Her mother had given her access to a trust from Maddy's grandparents that Maddy hadn't even known she'd had.

Maddy had a long way to go, but she was finally free. No one was after her. The Holts were facing serious time in prison. Their company was being investigated because of their ties to government officials in the biggest cover-up the state had seen. That meant her father was out of a job. He'd come crawling back to her mother, but Susan had held her ground and not taken him back.

Susan was still sober. Maddy and her mother wouldn't ever have the kind of relationship a mother and daughter were supposed to have. There was far too much bad blood between them. But Maddy allowed her in Josh's life as a grandparent—as long as Susan stayed sober.

Maddy turned the lights off as she went through the house. She grabbed the door handle to her room and pushed it open, her gaze landing on the man lying in bed with a book in his hands.

Turner's eyes flicked to hers before a smile illuminated his face. "Hey, gorgeous. How did it go?"

Maddy climbed into bed next to him, curling into his side. "I said my goodbyes. I just wish Hayley had told me when we were in school. It would have been nice to know I had a sister. Maybe things would have turned out differently."

He set the book on the bedside table and weaved his fingers inside hers. "I'm sorry."

She nodded. "It is what it is. I'm just glad you were okay."

Turner kissed her forehead. "Me too. A collapsed lung is no joke."

"You're lucky the bullet didn't hit anything vital."

He pulled back enough to meet her gaze. "It would take more than a bullet to keep me away from you, princess."

"Sweet talker," she teased with a smile.

He chuckled before his grin dimmed. "I'm sorry that I wasn't honest with you from the beginning."

"I think you've already apologized enough, don't you?" The last few months, Turner had done his best to make up for omitting the truth from her. He'd been an open book, willing to share whatever information Maddy wanted to know.

"Right, so where do we go from here?" he asked.

She tipped her chin up to kiss him softly on the lips. "We go forward."

His chest rumbled. "Mmm, I like the sound of that. You know the doctor cleared me for certain activities today."

Her eyebrows rose. "Oh, did he?"

Turner nodded, sliding his lips over hers as he climbed

over her. "So, what do you say, princess? Can I make love to you?"

Arousal pooled in her core. "You better."

He deepened the kiss, his sweet tongue gliding into her mouth as his hands made quick work of removing her sweater and bra. She shimmied out of them while he broke the kiss long enough to pull his own shirt off. She reached for his grey sweatpants, tugging them down. His cock sprang free, its head already leaking.

Cool air rushed over her legs as he bared herself to him. Goose bumps prickled her skin the way his heated gaze hungrily roamed over her like he was a man starved.

"You're so fucking beautiful."

Maddy sat on her knees, facing him in the same position. She wrapped her arms around his neck, kissing the red scar over his chest where he'd taken the bullet meant for her. Maddy fisted his cock, moving her hand up and down as she shuddered. His big, calloused hands roamed her body, squeezing her ass before he dipped two fingers inside her, his other hand squeezing her breast. She moaned. His mouth captured hers in a tangle of tongue and teeth, lips and mingled breaths.

Pleasure thrummed in her pussy. Her juices leaked down his hand, which was pumping in and out of her, and onto her thigh.

"Is this the spot, baby?" He curled his fingers, pressing the magic area that sent her body tensing under the building pressure in her core.

"Yes," she gasped.

"I want to feel you come on me. It's been too long."

His nose traced the edge of her jaw before he placed a light kiss on her shoulder, making her shiver.

"Lie down." She pushed his shoulders gently.

Turner slid backwards on the bed, sitting against the head-board before she climbed on his lap. Maddy lined up his cock and slid over him, engulfing his erection within her heat as flames of ecstasy licked her flesh in a carnal wildfire.

He hissed. "Fuuuuck. Yes. You feel so good. So hot and tight. I love your pussy."

She tilted her hips, rising and falling, riding him with slow purpose. Each thrust brought them closer and closer to shared heaven. He licked his thumb and pressed it to her clit, sending spikes of pleasure shooting through her body.

"Oh, God. Turner, I'm so close."

"Come for me, princess." Turner's gaze locked on to hers.

Her chest filled with warm elation, bursting from the dam in her heart. Love like she'd never known poured out until it radiated in every cell, breath, and plea leaving her lips.

"I love you so much." His other hand twisted her nipple, sending her over the edge. Her orgasm burst through her, shattering her in the best of ways. Maddy's breath hitched as he came with her, his ocean eyes locked on hers.

When she looked into his eyes—the windows to his soul—she could see her past and present crash in a beautiful colli-sion. All that remained was their future.

Thank you! We hope you enjoyed reading _Beautiful Collision_.

Curious about Jasmine and Atlas's story? Turn the page for a sneak peek of Chapter One in their book, **_The Lighthouse Inn_**.

Or visit the website below to order Book 4 in the Shattered Cove series right now.

WWW.AMKUSI.COM/THELIGHTHOUSEINN

If you prefer to read in order, start the series with book 1, *A Fallen Star.*

WWW.AMKUSI.COM/AFALLENSTAR

SNEAK PEEK OF THE LIGHTHOUSE INN: CHAPTER 1

Jasmine

Jasmine pulled the sheet over the two fluffy pillows, smoothing out the wrinkles before reaching for the soft, pink comforter. A paper card fell off the nightstand. Picking it up, she smiled. *Happy Mother's Day, Mommy!* The script no doubt belonged to one of her sisters-in-law, but the shakily scribbled Z's all over the card were from her favorite person in the world. Zoey had drawn two smiling faces: one for Jasmine and one for herself. Jasmine set the card back on the nightstand before running her hand over the bedspread once more. Never in a million years would she have imagined having such a feminine color in her space. Motherhood had changed more than just her body.

After tucking the edge of the comforter under the pillow, she moved across the small room she shared with her three-year-old daughter. She pulled open the old and worn dresser, wiggling it side to side at the same time so it wouldn't stick. Like everything in her life, it had been used almost beyond its limit. She placed Zoey's carefully folded clothes inside before wriggling it closed again. She scanned the room, catching the few dolls scattered across the floor. Jasmine bent and picked them up, opening the wooden dollhouse that Mikel, her brother, had made especially for Zoey. He'd painted it bright pink at her request. Jasmine bit back her smile. Only she would end up with such a girly girl for a daughter and be terrified.

She sighed, tracing the edge of the doll's expression. The two smiling faces on Zoey's Mother's Day card flashed in her mind. Her chest tightened. *Would Zoey have had a better life if I'd let someone adopt her? Would she have two parents who loved her, rather than just me? I can barely keep a roof over her head and used clothes on her quickly growing body.*

Maybe it had been selfish to keep Zoey, but the moment she'd seen that little heart beating on the ultrasound, she'd known: she'd never be able to give her up. *But will I be good enough? Will I be able to protect her? Will she resent me when she knows what I've done? Who I was?* Life would be so much easier if Jasmine was someone else with a different past.

The walls seemed to be closing in. Her ribs squeezed and the backs of her eyes burned. She gently placed the doll inside the wooden house and straightened. Taking a deep breath, she steadied herself. *I just need to keep doing better. For Zoey.* Her phone chirped, jarring her out of her thoughts. She had one guest checking in today, and that was what she should have been focusing on. She needed guests to keep her inn—her livelihood—afloat.

She wiped her hands on her ripped jean shorts that had seen better days and opened her door. As she walked down the stairs to the desk, a tall figure caught her eye. His back was to her, all attention focused on the painting of the crashing ocean waves on the wall.

"Good morning. You must be Mr. Remington."

A low chuckle sent a shiver through her. "My father is Mr. Remington. I'm just Atlas."

She smiled politely as her eyes darted to his face, and she froze. Time stopped. The air evaporated as terror gripped her heart and squeezed it like a vise. His tall frame filled out an expensive-looking suit. His black hair was long at the top and flecked with grey at the shorter sides. Dark scruff peppered his perfectly chiseled jaw. She shivered, remembering the way it had felt brushing across her shoulder. And those eyes. Grey and bright. She only knew one other person with the same cloudy orbs. *Zoey.*

He'd changed some in the last four years since she'd seen him. Not that she'd had much time to really look at him before she'd nodded towards the dingy bathroom in the bar where he'd followed her and bent her over the sink. Flames of embarrassment lapped at her skin. She'd been looking for an escape that night, and the stranger had been more than willing to help.

Atlas. Atlas Remington. She finally had a name for Zoey's biological father.

"What are you doing here?" She gasped. Was he here to take Zoey from her? Had he known all this time? *No.* That wasn't possible. No one knew what had happened in that bathroom except them.

His eyebrows furrowed. "Uh, checking in. I should have a reservation for two weeks."

Did he not recognize her? Was it possible? He'd smelled strongly of whiskey that night. Maybe he had no idea who she was.

"Right. Sorry. We don't know each other, do we?" She held her breath.

"I think I'd remember if we did." He smiled. Was he flirting with her?

"What are you in town for?" she asked carefully, finding his paperwork.

He looked around the room at the high, white patched ceiling and then over to the paint-chipped furniture, rather than at her before he answered. "Just needed a little vacation."

"And you chose my inn? Was it my two Yelp reviews that convinced you?" She couldn't hold back her smile.

He chuckled again. Those grey eyes flashing as they focused on her. "I like the location and wanted to see it for myself. The pictures didn't do it justice though."

Her eyes flicked down momentarily. "Well, someday I'll hire a professional photographer."

"Oh, no. The pictures were great. I just meant it's even better in person." He smiled, showing off his perfect, white teeth. Good God. Was he a toothpaste model?

"Do you need my credit card?" he asked.

Shit. She'd been staring. "Uh, no. It's all on file. Just sign here." She pointed to the space on the form ready and waiting on the counter. "You have the Lighthouse suite like you requested. There are extra towels in the closet in the bathroom. I'll come in to clean every three days unless you need it done sooner—just let me know."

He nodded and scribbled his signature on the paper. Jasmine held out the lone key ring with a lighthouse chain and his receipt. "I'll charge the card you provided when booking with any incidentals. Your room is just up the stairs to the left." *Across from mine.* "There's a sign on the door. The silver key works for the front door, and the brass key is for your room. Did you need more than one set, or will it just be you staying with us?"

"Just me. The one is fine." He took it from her and

reached to grab a duffel bag she hadn't noticed in the shock of seeing her baby daddy from a one-night stand—if you could even call it that. Were ten-minute stands a thing?

"Enjoy your stay. I leave my number at the desk here." She pointed to the folded card stock sign right next to the one stating *No cash kept on premises.* "And it's also on the copy of your receipt. Just text me if you need anything and I'm not at the front desk."

"You run the inn by yourself?"

She smiled with pride. "Yes, I do."

He nodded and grabbed the papers before walking towards the stairs. She waited until the click of his door closing sounded to let out the breath she'd been holding.

"Holy fucking shit." She placed a shaky hand over her racing heart as if it would help to calm the panic.

She whipped out her phone and stepped into the large kitchen, dialing her big brother Bently's number.

He picked up on the second ring. "Hey, Jas. You on your way?"

She swallowed hard before answering. Jasmine didn't need her brother freaking out and showing up here to make things worse. Even she didn't know what the hell was going on yet. "Uh, no. Actually, I need you to keep Zoey overnight."

"Is everything okay?" The concern in his voice brought a rush of guilt crashing over her.

Not even close to okay. Of all the people in her life, Bently had been the one constant—the only person she could count on. She hated to lie, but she'd brought enough trouble to their family. No. She'd handle this on her own.

"I have everything under control, Bent. I just need you to do this and not ask me any questions. Okay? I'll owe you one." More like a million, but who was counting?

"Okay. Fine. Anything you need," Bently said.

"Thank you. I'll call before bed to say goodnight to her."

"Sounds good." Bently ended the call.

Jasmine opened her contacts. She needed to talk to someone about this. But her best friend, Remy, was married to Mikel, and she was shit at keeping secrets from him. The last thing Jasmine wanted was her two overprotective brothers jumping in to save her. *Again.* She'd caused them all enough pain. This was her doing and she would fix this. *Somehow.*

She scrolled through her contacts until Emma's name popped up and hit call before she could back out. It rang and rang until her friend picked up.

"Jazzy! Hey, mama. I got a quick break from the studio. How are you?" Emma asked as background music filtered through the phone.

Jasmine covered her mouth with her hand, trying to quiet the sob that surprised even her.

"Jas? What's wrong? Are you okay?" Emma asked. The noise grew quieter, as if she'd moved away.

"He's here," she managed.

"Who's there?"

"Zoey's father. He's staying at my inn."

Emma was silent for a few beats. "Is this a good thing or a bad thing?"

She couldn't blame her friend for not knowing. There were several things Jasmine kept locked away in a vault of topics she wouldn't talk about. Zoey's biological father was one of them. She was too ashamed.

"I don't know, honestly." Jasmine wiped the tears from her eyes and walked out to the back deck. Salty sea air blew gently over her skin as waves crashed in the distance.

"Okay. Does he know about Zoey?"

"I don't even think he remembers me."

"Oh, sweetie."

"I—I don't know what to do." Jasmine shook her head.

"I wish I could offer advice, but you have never said anything about this guy."

Jasmine sighed. "I know. It's a part of my past that I'd like to omit. I did a lot of fucked-up things, and I'd just rather forget the girl I used to be."

"I get it . . . So, can you explain how you made a baby with him, but he somehow can't recognize you?" Emma asked carefully.

Flashes came back of that dark bar. Those grey eyes had burned her skin with awareness, making it clear exactly what he'd wanted from her before he'd ever even offered to buy her a drink.

"He was just a guy from a bar. We never exchanged names, just . . . body fluids."

"Thanks for the mental image," Emma said and laughed. "Is he hot?"

Jasmine rolled her eyes. "On a one-to-ten scale, he's an eleven."

"Damn, girl. So, how can this godlike man not recognize you? Tell me it was something kinky like a sex party with masks."

Jasmine laughed. Only Emma could take a subject like this and turn it into something to laugh about. "It was less than ten minutes in a bathroom and I never saw him again . . . until today."

"Was it a good ten minutes?" Emma asked.

Jasmine blew out through her nose. "It was . . . okay." Achieving orgasm with a partner was pretty rare for her. Zoey's father hadn't been one of those unicorn moments.

"Hot but not great in the sack. Got it. Well, we can't all be perfect. Maybe you should try sleeping with a woman; I've never not had an orgasm with a woman. With guys, it's fifty-fifty."

"I wish I could be sexually attracted to a woman." They seemed safer.

"Okay, so maybe it is a good thing your baby daddy is back in your life," Emma suggested.

Jasmine paced back and forth over the long porch. "How exactly?"

"You can get to know him and see if he's a decent guy. Maybe Zoey can have her dad in her life after all."

Jasmine stopped, a rush of dizziness spinning though her head. She sat on the ground with her head lowered to her knees. "I'm scared. What if he tries to take her from me? What if he says I'm a bad mom? What if—"

"What if he's a great father? What if Zoey could have two parents in her life? What if he can help provide for her and take some of that stress off you?"

Jasmine blinked back more tears. She hated showing her emotions like this, but that was something else that mother-hood had changed. She couldn't hide anymore.

Emma had a point. Jasmine wouldn't let fear stand in the way of Zoey's chances of happiness. If Atlas was a good father, and she didn't try, then she'd be robbing Zoey of some-thing Jasmine herself had never had but always wanted. She couldn't hold the man's sexual history against him. After all, she'd done the same thing—more than once.

"You're right. I'll get to know him. I'll see if he's a safe person, observe how good he is with Zoey. Then I'll tell him."

"I'm here for you. Whatever you need," Emma offered.

"Thank you. I appreciate it. Can you keep this between us for now? I don't want Remy to find out just yet. She'll tell Mikel and then—"

"And then you'll have two big brothers and their best

friend knocking on your door and getting into the middle of your business. I got you."

Jasmine laughed. "They probably wouldn't even knock. They'd bust the thing down."

Emma giggled. "True. Well, I know they have your back, but I also respect your right as Zoey's mother to do what you think is right."

"You're the best, Em."

"Tell that to my stepbrother the next time you see him." Emma laughed again, but this time it sounded forced.

"I'll mention it to Link," Jasmine promised. It was a hopeless cause, much to her friend's dismay.

"Okay, well, I gotta get back. Almost done with this album and then I start my tour next week," Emma said.

"I'm so happy that your dream is becoming a reality. Soon you'll be too famous to be my friend."

"Never!"

"Talk to you later." Jasmine smiled.

"Love you, bitch."

"You too." Jasmine slipped the phone in her back pocket and got to her feet once more.

Taking a deep breath, she stared past the tall beach grass and rose hip bushes towards the expanse of green-blue waves. They crashed against the rocks to her left and licked the sandy coast to her right as the ocean tide worked its way in. She could do this. For Zoey, she'd do anything. If that meant giving her father a chance, she'd do it. And if it meant keeping who he was a secret for the rest of her time on earth, she'd do that too.

Because Zoey would not go through the shit she'd been through. Jasmine would work through the pain of the past so that her daughter didn't have to have one-tenth of the trauma in her life that Jasmine had had. She'd protect her daughter, no matter what it took. Jasmine knew better than anyone that of all the people in a child's life, the father figure could be the most dangerous.

To continue reading Jasmine and Atlas's story, visit the website below to get your copy of *The Lighthouse Inn* today.

WWW.AMKUSI.COM/THELIGHTHOUSEINN

JOIN OUR NEWSLETTER

The best way to get updates about new releases, sneak peeks, pre-orders, giveaways, and more is by joining our newsletter.

You'll also receive a FREE story that's not available on any retailer to read.

Visit the website below to join now.

WWW.AMKUSI.COM/NEWSLETTER

THANK YOU

Thank you for reading *Beautiful Collision*. We hope you are emotionally satisfied with Maddy and Turner's love story. If you enjoyed this novel, please consider leaving a review on your favorite retailer and sharing it with your friends and family.

If you haven't read Remy and Mikel's story yet, check out **A Fallen Star** (Book 1 in The Shattered Cove Series. The eBook is FREE on all retailers.)

For Andre and Mia's story, check out **Glass Secrets** (Book 2 in The Shattered Cove Series)

For Belle and Bently's story, check out **Defying Gravity** (Book 3 in The Shattered Cove Series)

For Jasmine and Atlas, check out **The Lighthouse Inn** (Book 4 in The Shattered Cove Series)

For Charli and Finn, check out **His True North** (Book 5 in The Shattered Cove Series)

For Emma and Link, check out **In The Grey** (Book 6 in The Shattered Cove Series)

For Mason and Pippa, check out **Brave Love** (Book 7 in The Shattered Cove Series)

Lastly, if you haven't read our debut series, **The Orchard Inn Romance Series**, make sure you get your copy so you don't miss out on three wonderful love stories.

Thank you again for reading *Beautiful Collision!*

Cheers,

Ash & Marcus.

ABOUT A. M. KUSI

A. M. Kusi is the pen name of a wife-and-husband team, Ash and Marcus Kusi. We enjoy writing emotional romance novels that are inspired by our experiences as an interracial/multicultural couple.

Our novels are about strong women and the sexy heroes they fall in love with, are emotionally satisfying, and always have a happy ending.

Discover more about us at:

WWW.AMKUSI.COM

To receive updates about new releases, preorders, giveaways, and more, visit the website below to join our newsletter today:

WWW.AMKUSI.COM/NEWSLETTER

After you join the newsletter, we will send you a FREE story to read.

To contact us, use this email address: amkusinovels@gmail.com

Happy reading!

Ash and Marcus

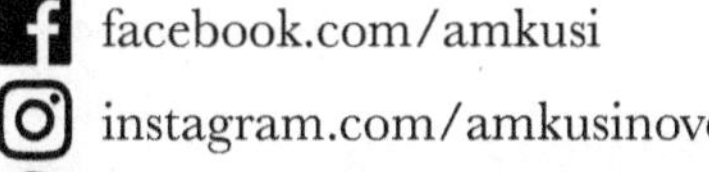

facebook.com/amkusi

instagram.com/amkusinovels

pinterest.com/amkusinovels

ALSO BY A. M. KUSI

A Fallen Star (eBook FREE on all retailers)

(Book 1 in The Shattered Cove Series)

Glass Secrets

(Book 2 in The Shattered Cove Series)

Defying Gravity

(Book 3 in The Shattered Cove Series)

The Lighthouse Inn

(Book 4 in The Shattered Cove series)

His True North

(Book 5 in The Shattered Cove series)

In The Grey

(Book 6 in The Shattered Cove series)

Brave Love

(Book 7 in The Shattered Cove series)

The Orchard Inn (eBook FREE on all retailers)

(Book 1 in The Orchard Inn Romance Series)

Conflict of Interest

(Book 2 in The Orchard Inn Romance Series)

Her Perfect Storm

(Book 3 in The Orchard Inn Romance Series)

One Holiday Kiss (eBook FREE on all retailers)

(A Shattered Cove Short Story)

For a complete list of all our books, visit:

WWW.AMKUSI.COM/BOOKS